Odd bird the fish

Mark Calland

Published by New Generation Publishing in 2024

First Edition

ISBN   978-1-83563-163-8

www.newgeneration-publishing.com

New Generation Publishing

For C, E and J

Uncontrollably, in great rollicking spasms, like the sea.

Dylan Moran

1

Sunday 26 September 2010

Here we are, yet once more, my daughters and I, on an underground journey across London, as the bittersweet pleasure of a Sunday afternoon slides into the shadows of Sunday evening.

With a cursory glance, the thirty-something woman opposite us has, no doubt, assessed our situation and concluded that we're provincials scrambling back across the capital from a shabby, overpriced hotel with our broken-handled trolley case. Her neutral expression betrays no benign appreciation of how endearing a trio we might be.

As seasoned Tube riders, the girls had slipped into their customary blasé, self-contained mode and almost simultaneously taken out their books and started reading. Does she think they're freaks or is she, as a fellow bookworm, secretly filled with admiration? Left bank combat, you might call her style—Bohemian chic with a nod to the Clash.

I catch sight of the reflection of a face in the window beside her and for an instant fail to recognize the man on the Daddies sauce bottles looking blankly back at me. That's me. I have become the man on the Daddies sauce bottles.

Was the Daddies sauce man even balding though? Am I someone who is even on the wrong side of aspiring to adequately convey an air of comfortable, avuncular middle age?

Biology had dictated that no sooner had I stopped getting spots than my hairline started to recede and the hair that was being lost from my head seemed to correspond directly with the hair that was sprouting unsolicited in my ears, nostrils, eyebrows and on my chest. It seems that, in some cases, we humans skip very swiftly from development to decline and, are, in effect, destined in most cases to spend the majority of our lives past our prime.

Left bank is looking pretty good, though—somehow you can tell she's probably older than she looks.

Half-completed yesterday's Guardian cryptic. Has she spotted mine conspicuously sticking out of my coat pocket, I wonder? She looks like she's not taking us in, but she's probably sketched out a whole scenario in her head. That's what normal people do, apparently—project stories onto things. They do it about the future too, constantly running through how things might pan out. Mapping things out. Fantasising.

I never do that. Not in a positive way at least. I might suddenly cut to a nightmare scenario in a situation I'm dreading, but it's not in any great detail and, more often than not, it's just an overall vague sense of dread itself.

Aren't us chaps supposed to have just a vague but pervading sense of impending success or increased popularity? The happy self-delusion of youth; a life-long survival tool for some.

I remember as a child before a 'big' football match that I was playing in, trying a positive visualisation technique by endeavouring to imagine myself taking a successful penalty, but no matter how many times I tried to force the ball into the net, it just wouldn't go in. I never once managed to score.

Liverpool Street. Makes me think of the colour orange for some reason. Is it an orange card in Monopoly? Do the train stations have colours? Is it even one of the stations?

Funny how orange isn't a more popular colour, seeing as it is generally associated with the sun, fruit and summer and has positive, warm and bright connotations. I don't think I've ever heard anyone say that it's their favourite colour. Most people don't seem to like ginger hair—which is, in effect, orange—either. Why don't we just say orange?

My daughters' hair is definitely getting a bit gingerish, or auburny at least. They're getting a bit freckly now too—a sprinkle of summer across their noses.

As I know they would be embarrassed, I have to resist the temptation to press the palm of my hand down softly on the crowns of their heads or to lean over and breathe in the faint baby smell that still lingers from where their fontanelles once were. I smell of peanuts apparently.

Are they different when they're with their mum? I will probably never know. Sometimes when we were all on the Tube and Rachel and I couldn't sit together, we would catch each other's eye across the carriage; on the surface archly enjoying this intimate detachment, but also putting each other into perspective again in the crowd. I always thought that she would be thinking, *If I didn't know him, I'm pretty sure I wouldn't be attracted to him. Can that be right?*

We roll on in silence, deep under the ground. You can almost imagine the train just carrying on and on, never reaching any stations and nobody batting an eyelid, just gently jostling on, blank-faced along an interminable tunnel. You could imagine someone making a short, existentialist Nordic film along those lines.

A metaphor for modern life.

A good idea. But what's the point?

We're moving through the intestines of London. The bowels of the behemoth, via peristalsis.

There's a poem in there. T.S. Eliot or Roger McGough? Could go either way.

'Each stop a colon'—that would definitely be the latter.

You would need to find a better word than 'moving' though—something intestinal. McGough would probably call it *The Underground Movement.*

Maybe I could work the idea of a hollow wind into it—the wind that hits you when you're walking along the tunnels sometimes. Is hollow wind right for that, though? The Tube wind is warm.

'*Hollow wind, hollow cheeks*' or '*Hollow wind, hollow faces*'? '*Faces*' sounds more ghostly somehow.

3

'Hollow wind, hollow faces. Thinking myself hollow.'

Somebody must have used *hollow wind* before.

The mother and son opposite have the same eyes. Like amused mice. Can you see the ghost of his father in his face by mentally subtracting the mother's features? In theory. Be interesting to see. Following them home in the hope of seeing the father would be taking it a bit too far. I wonder what it's like following someone though. It can't be easy. Depends who it is, I suppose. Some people are oblivious to most things going on around them. I wonder if I've ever been followed and not realised?

I sometimes vary my routes to work just in case. Is that crazy? And stand with my back right up against the wall on train platforms so that nobody can push me in front of the train. Looking out for people with suspicious backpacks on and changing carriages at the next stop if I spot one. A white flash, a bang and we would all be gone.

How did I get like this?

I suppose it's partly a game; pretending I'm in the *Ipcress File* or something, but it does seem like there's always been a war going on in the background here. As soon as Northern Ireland was sorted out and the threat of the IRA receded, along came Al Qaeda…

You could argue that I'm being irresponsible bringing the girls on the Tube. I drove them for a while, but you're statistically more likely to die in a car crash and it's no friend of the environment. And one of the bomb attacks was on a bus…

I get it from my parents too. Mum and Dad have both had their bouts of paranoia.

He said they would be throwing bricks through the window. And then her post-natal depression—or post-partum psychosis as they would call it now—when she thought the IRA were after my dad.

Why did she sleep on the floor of my room that night and how come he let her? Maybe she slipped out of their bed after he'd fallen asleep.

I kept darts under the mattress. I used to feel ashamed of that. Or am I more ashamed now? It's hard to check on yourself, but how else do you check? See a psychiatrist, I suppose.

When I was fifteen, a psychiatrist was charged with the routine task of deciding whether I was sane or not — in a half-hour session.

'Would you say that you worried about things a lot?'

'No more than anyone else.'

'I see you're moving those crumbs around on the table. Do you like to have things in order?'

'Not particularly.'

And with those carefully weighted answers, I was spared a possible lifetime of secure psychiatric units. The psychiatrist didn't seem to care one way or another.

I'll have to tell the girls one day. Poor things. Daddy is tainted. But it will fade. Everything fades. Like the light from a dead star. You can see it, but it isn't there anymore. You can observe it, but you can't feel it. Time is a healer, but it's also a killer. Good things die over time. Good feelings. Like when you hear a favourite song and it doesn't give you the same feeling of visceral excitement that it used to anymore, so you ration out your special songs for fear of them dying on you.

It's the same with books. If it's a good one, I'll stretch it out for as long as I can.

Rachel was the opposite. She'd just race through it. She'd race through any book or just abandon it if she couldn't get into it. I hate finishing a great book because it's like leaving another world behind forever. Of course, you can go back in and read it again a bit later, but it's not the same—you're not the same.

The kids can instantly get lost in their Harry Potter books, no matter where they are. They seem to find the Tube strangely soothing. Maybe there's something foetal about it? Or maybe it's not so cosy being in the womb after all. Perhaps it's a profound, familiarly unsettling uterine feeling that's merely sedating rather than comforting them?

It's interesting how there are all these books dissecting thoughts and ideas, but hardly anything on feelings. They're mostly overlooked intellectually, although we would be automatons without them. The oversight is understandable, though, as feelings are so nebulous, but they're arguably the prime motivators in life, and the moments when you feel most alive, regardless of whether they're positive or negative. They're like the flippers, bumpers and return lane of a pinball machine—the things that make the game worth playing. Without them, life would be like bagatelle. I wonder what major new feelings I will experience before I head down the out lane and into the out hole. Not many, really—probably just two main ones, one of which is desirable, but highly unlikely—the euphoria of major success, and the other is any sane parent's most dreaded feeling… Your blood runs cold just at the thought of it.

Maybe this is why feelings are intermittent; you'd be exhausted if you were experiencing thousands of subtle variations of them all the time for every slightly different situation. Maybe some people do. Maybe it's a condition that some people have. Would that be a blessing or a curse?

Does the mind rule the body or does the body rule the mind? I don't know.

Blackfriars.

An evocative name. It has built-in atmosphere. A lot of the names of the stations on this line are architectural or classical sounding. *Monument*, *Temple*. Cold and self-important. Make me think of paintings by Poussin or Claude Lorrain.

Three gates, a Barbican and an Embankment. Not the most attractive of names. Unlike *Piccadilly Circus* or *Pimlico*—I wonder where that comes from? It sounds like a mixture between a pinstriped Whitehall mandarin and a resort on the Amalfi coast. Interesting that I like the ones with a foreign ring.

Have always loved the street name Portobello Road. Some names are very evocative, very atmospheric. Atmosphere is an interesting phenomenon. Do all places have an atmosphere of sorts? It seems to me that they do. Or maybe I'm just extra-sensitive to it? Maybe we do have feelings all the time after all, but they are mainly just a sense of the 'atmosphere' we're experiencing. I get cowed by changes in atmosphere and can find them intimidating, whereas some people just seem to be able to override them. Maybe this is just what shyness is—not having a portable sense of yourself that you can effortlessly export to most situations. If you overcame your shyness, would you also lose the sensitivity to all those feelings linked to places, because even the environments that inhibit you can at the same time engender a lovely feeling or 'sense' of the place? Sometimes the most powerful and attractive 'sense' of a place that you experience is actually somewhere that you've never actually been to; a place and a time that you have read about in a novel or history book or which might have been conjured up in a song or seen in a film or TV show— a sort of seminal Shangri-La that you always yearn in vain to experience in real life.

The mother and child are getting off. She shrugs her bag into position and is gone.

There goes my beautiful world...

That was where our paths crossed. She's the star, I'm the extra. I'm the star, she's the extra. Everywhere is the centre of the universe...

We're all equal on the Tube. That's one of the reasons some people hate public transport. They're secretly against national identity cards for the same reason. It's not just the invasion of privacy argument, it's the fact that it makes us all seem like equal citizens, with a photo and a number.

Baronet Sir Thomas Slingsby doesn't want to have to suffer the indignity of carrying one around and to have to produce it on demand like an immigrant forced to prove their residency status.

It's all about freedom rather than equality these days. Freedom and choice. The freedom to be privileged. And the privileged are prepared to fight harder to hold on to their privilege than the deprived are to escape their deprivation.

Something in between might be the best solution—a happy medium. Hard to get people excited about that though. Heroic moderation! Not exactly going to get the masses rushing to the barricades…

How did I get onto that? *Cognitive concatenation* — train of thought.

Sometimes things just seem to pop into your head for no reason, though. And it's often the same seemingly inconsequential moments again and again… Coming home from school along Ladysmith Avenue back in Yewton, past the gas showrooms. Grey sky, night falling—must have been autumn or winter. A gloomy feeling.

I think I was wondering whether the other kids thought about what they were going to say in advance of social situations. Whether they tried to slip funny things that they had thought of earlier into the conversation or simply just winged it. They seemed so relaxed about it all, but how do you know that you're going to be able to think of anything funny to say when you meet up? You don't, so how can you not worry about that? Did they think like me or did they think differently?

I think that was what I was thinking about at that moment, but retrospectively, the actual feeling was, I think, one of alienation. I probably didn't even know the word then.

Strangely, I think I can remember the exact moment I used it for the first time, though, several years later. I was back from uni for Christmas and had been out drinking with my friends from home. We were walking along by the park and I confided in Alan that I still felt alienated. I was simultaneously embarrassed at my arty pretentiousness and yet hopeful of impressing him with my intellectualism. He reacted well, I seem to remember. Took it in his stride.

I might even have been wearing the beret that Kate had bought me. And that reefer jacket. Trying to be all Greenwich Village.

I lived with them on Montague Street in the basement down the stairs
Music in the cafes at night and revolution in the air

Even Dylan never resorted to a beret, as far as I'm aware.

Nobody took the mick, though. Not like when I wore the straw boater, but actually, even then, Rachel only took the mick retrospectively. She probably didn't feel she knew me well enough at the time—it was still the very early days.

I've always thought that I was very self-conscious, but I did have the nerve to wear a beret and a straw boater—if nerve is the right word. I almost certainly wore them self-consciously though.

I remember the first time I heard the word 'self-conscious'. My dad was commenting on John Lennon in the film where the Beatles all live next door to each other in a row of terraced houses that share the same space inside but have separate front doors. How old was I then? It was in Yewton, so I must have been at least seven.

Is this normal? I used to remember everything. Clear and sharp. Weirdly, it felt like a kind of burden though. There was no escape. I used to yearn for a bit of oblivion, a bit of vagueness, but now the haziness is starting to kick in, it's a bit disconcerting. I almost want the constant clarity back. The lack of sleep you get when the kids are little is doubtless what triggers the decline.

I've always liked impressing my mum with insignificant details from my childhood, but she often seems slightly uncomfortable and disturbed by it. Probably because it suggests that I remember other things too…

If I were Rachel now, I would be thinking about the kids' dental appointments or what to get my brother for his birthday. Am I just self-obsessed? Is that what it is? I'm not sure. Just another part of the autistic licence that she said she granted me. Maybe.

If you're sitting on a Tube train with your daughters and are thinking of a scenario, for example, where the Tube line just keeps going gradually down and down to hell as the train gathers speed and the passengers start to perspire and eye each other with concern as it gets hotter and hotter before finally the train disappears through the sliding doors of a huge cremation furnace and then automatically assume that it must have been thought of before, does that make you self-absorbed? Maybe. Immature? Probably. A concern? Who knows? Surely out of all the tens of millions of people who have travelled regularly on the Tube, a fair few must have had thoughts along those lines?

Which Tube station could have a witty, cryptic reference to hell in its name? Burnt Oak? Blackfriars? You fry and turn black. Sounds both sinister and ecclesiastical.

I definitely don't want to be cremated. But how will anyone know that? Wear a tag? Write '*Please don't cremate me!*' in permanent marker pen across my chest? I could die in a fire though. I wonder if they ever cremate partially burned remains? Finish the job off. *Chard remains our destination.*

It's adding insult to injury though, isn't it? Imagine doing that for a living. Do they burn the coffins too? Bet they don't. Flog them off again probably. Maybe you can just rent them and then they don't actually burn the casket.

How can people know for sure that they're getting their loved one's ashes? They probably just have a big tub of the stuff and scoop some out into an urn for each funeral.

Better to be buried. At least you feel you're part of the circle of life, nourishing the soil, being meat for worms... *Putting something back at grassroots level.* If you are cremated, you're just creating pollution.

I wonder if this line runs under any graveyards—some lines must do. Travelling under the dead. '*Under the dead*'—a good title.

The proliferation of people on the surface is such that we now burrow our way across town to our destinations through a network of tunnels, the dead stretched out above us...

It's pushed to the back of your mind most of the time, but sometimes it just stops you in your tracks.

There's that moment in everyone's childhood when it hits you with a sick sense of dread and panic that your parents are going to die one day, but you don't think about it happening to yourself until later. Then, when you have kids, you realise that there might be thirty years of their lives that you will miss and have no idea about and it just kills you. It'll all carry on without you and you won't be able to share any of their highs or lows.

The whole mortality thing didn't really hit me properly until I read *Nausea,* aged nineteen, but I remember Mr Fox at primary school asking us when we thought that humans start to die, and answering, *'About nineteen, when we stop growing?'*, only to be told that it was, in fact, from the day we are born. With each second from then on, we are getting a step closer to death.

I don't think he liked me; neither did the headmaster.

'You're a funny boy, Roche.'

My mum went mad when I told her he had said that. I wished I hadn't told her, but I was also pleased that she was angry with him and was being protective of me.

She was always the protective one, rushing to our defence if the neighbours accused us of something. My dad would always try and be fair and see it from their side too, but you couldn't help feeling sort of betrayed by his even-handedness.

'Is it five more stops, Daddy?'

'I don't know. Let's have a look. 1, 2, 3, 4... 5. Yes, well done, Becky!'

I glance at a poster for the London 2012 Olympics next to the Tube map and hope that the kids haven't got wind of the Bart and Lisa Simpson resemblance as they might be tempted to ask me about it. What a truly terrible design it is. There is also absolutely nothing British about it either, in the colour scheme or design. It's almost as if someone deliberately came up with the worst logo possible for a laugh and threw in a hidden obscene dimension to boot, just to see if they could get away with it. Hats off to you, mystery marketing execs—you pulled it off!

'Daddy, there's a purse on the floor over there'.

She was right. Over by the doors.

'Should we pick it up and hand it in, Daddy?'

Someone else might not be as honest as us.

'Yes, I think we should.'

So, I very self-consciously go over and get it. Most of the other passengers are making out that they're not interested or paying attention, but Rive Gauche opposite gives us a little smile of approval. Now, there's one who knows how to rock a beret—she could probably even carry off a raspberry one too.

Some of the other onlookers will, no doubt, be wondering whether I'm going to keep it, but they'll all be wondering how much money there is in it and whether I'm going to open it now and have a look.

Would it look more like I was going to keep it if I opened it up now or if I just hold it in my hand. Or should I just put it straight into my pocket?

I can feel the corners of their ostensibly indifferent eyes upon me.

'Are we going to hand it in at the ticket office, Daddy?'

'Yes, we are, darling. Or at least they will be able to tell us where we can hand it in.'

'Shall we open it and see whose it is?'

'No, it's private, darling. We'll just make sure that it gets to the lost property office.'

And I just hold it there conspicuously in my hand until we get off.

18

When they got off at High Street Ken, only one woman from the same carriage got off with them. It wasn't her normal stop, but the situation was such that she couldn't resist—she felt a bit giddy and restless inside and in need of more of a walk anyway.

As she walked a little way behind them, she tried to picture what she would have imagined his face to look like if she didn't already know, but couldn't quite manage it.

She had often tried to guess whether someone she was walking behind was good-looking or not—with mixed results.

As he stepped onto the escalator, she got a full rear view of him and noticed that he had sat in some chocolate or something.

She wasn't that bothered about that part of the male anatomy and had been known to point out to friends admiring one that they found particularly impressive that shit came out of it. This looked more like a chocolate button, though.

She was also curious to see what he would do with the purse, and when they reached the concourse, she saw him and the girls pause at the queue for the ticket office, so she pretended to browse at a souvenir shop as they joined the queue.

When he suddenly looked round towards her, she quickly feigned interest in the tacky pomp and circumstance of the mini Big Bens and phone box key rings before moving across to the tourist postcards.

When she ventured another sideways look about thirty seconds later, she couldn't see them and stepped sharply out to get a better view before hurrying across to the nearest exit.

The shop owner, meanwhile, a vigilant looking man in his fifties, had made a mental note of her manoeuvre. She was definitely up to something. He wondered how he might describe her to the police.

Mid-thirtiess, pretty, continental-looking, about five foot seven, wearing a beret and a kind of smartish donkey jacket. And the guy she was following was with two little girls with reddish hair. He was maybe late thirties, slim, average height. Looked familiar. Someone from an advert maybe?

4

Calum Roche's kitchen overlooked a small garden, which backed onto a park. There were no blinds on the large window and sometimes when he padded around in there at night with the light on, he would peer out into the gloom and imagine the sudden thud of an assassin's silenced bullet punching into his forehead and sending him sprawling backwards across the room.

He was a sitting duck and if it happened on a Friday night, it could be days before his body was discovered.

He pictured himself from outside through the killer's sights—on display, fully exposed. Sometimes he'd leave the main light off and potter around in the light cast by the open fridge.

The strange thing was that at the same time he didn't fear the bullet—he sensed that it would punch satisfyingly into the centre of his forehead; like a bus conductor punching your ticket. It would be a kind of consummation; *a consummation devoutly to be wished.*

He hadn't had time to hand the purse in that day—there was too much of a queue at the ticket office and he was already late dropping the kids off at their mum's— but as soon as he'd got home afterwards, he'd gone through everything, looking for a way of contacting the person. He couldn't help feeling slightly uncomfortable about what he was doing, even though he knew it was perfectly innocent. The purse had a small embossed symbol on it, which looked like a simple figure of a man with his arms by his side and a sort of plectrum-shaped ring for a head. There were a couple of bank cards in the name of Anna Aharoni inside and an ID card with a picture of her wearing a headscarf. A bit of change and an invoice, which looked like it was addressed to her, and a passport photo of a little boy, whom he presumed was her son.

There wasn't much to go on. She could be a diplomat's wife. She could be mixed up in something dodgy. Maybe he would be getting mixed up in something he shouldn't be? He google-imaged her but her face didn't match any of the few Anna Aharonis that came up.

The landline rang. He almost never answered his landline blind and let it ring out until the answerphone clicked on as usual. A female voice.

'Oh, hi. I'm trying to contact Calum Roche because I think I've found his wallet on the Tube. Give me a call back on 0 2 0 3 1 9 18 1 13.'

His wallet was sitting on the kitchen table beside him. What was going on? It couldn't be a weird wind-up as he hadn't told anybody about finding a purse—unless the girls had mentioned it to their mum (they were bound to have done) and she'd got someone to phone up. It didn't sound like her putting a voice on though, and it would be really out of character for her to do something like this. Very fishy, though.

He listened to the message again. The way that she said the phone number was strange. He played it again and wrote the number down.

'O. Two. O. Three. One. Nine. Eighteen. One. Thirteen.'
He then phoned it.

'*The number you have dialled has not been recognised.*'

He dialled again with the same result. He then tried 1471 but the number had been withheld.

He listened to the message again and checked whether he'd written it down correctly. He had. Then he counted the numbers. There were eleven.

It crossed his mind that it was some kind of code and that this was a wind-up of a different kind. He'd been round at his friend Alastair's a few months before and they'd been flicking through the channels and started watching *The Da Vinci Code* and taking the mick out of it. But Ally couldn't know that he'd found a purse—unless he was in touch with

Rachel, which was highly unlikely. She had no time for Ally at all. Why would she even mention something so trivial anyway, even if she had happened to bump into him? And not enough time had elapsed anyway.

He gave Ally a ring, but couldn't get through and when he tried to text him, the message failed to send.

He looked at the mystery number he'd written down and then stared out at the lone tree in the garden that was being stirred by the autumn breeze like an orchestra being conducted by an invisible maestro.

He'd watched a Turkish film a few nights before in which the camera had lingered for a long time on a tree swaying in the wind. Somehow it had seemed to capture the sad, beautiful essence of being alive, but looking at this actual real tree before him now, though he could admire the wistful beauty of the scene, he couldn't feel it—he could see it, but he couldn't feel it. He just felt the loneliness of another solitary Sunday evening.

He'd messed things up. By being complacent and a misery. He would probably slowly drift apart from the girls over time too. They wouldn't want to come and stay with him when they were teenagers. He could already see it starting to happen with Molly—she only really wanted to stay one night most of the time.

He stood there staring at the bittersweet arboreal dance for a little while longer.

A cluster of leaves fluttered off here and there like scattering birds.

13

Monday

Having failed to contact Alastair by phone, Calum decided to call in on him on the way home from work. Ally was his oldest friend and had come down to London a couple of years before he had.

They'd been in the same class at school and formed a bedroom band together in their late teens, but then drifted apart somewhat as Ally had got heavily into drugs and family life had taken over for Calum. Since the split with Rachel, however, they'd started to see a bit more of each other and it seemed that Ally had now restricted his narcotic consumption to a more recreational—rather than industrial—level.

If Calum was honest, he would have to say that, overall, he'd found adult male friendship disappointing. Maybe his expectations had been unrealistic, but it had rarely lived up to the ideal of camaraderie that he'd seen in films, or matched the deep, primal attachment to his family that he'd felt at certain times. As he got older, he had even started to suspect that being with friends made him feel less real, less alive than when he was on his own. He felt as if there was a thick, watery membrane between him and others in social situations that he couldn't break through. It was an involuntary version of when Benjamin Braddock in *The Graduate* stays under the water in the swimming pool for a while and can hear the remote voices and see the broken shapes of people interacting above him. The membrane would become thinner as he got to know people, but only seldom fully disappeared. He really wanted to feel that bond with a friend again, like when he was young.

What made it harder with Alastair was that they'd both changed during the long gaps in their relationship, and nostalgia for the halcyon days could only stretch so far – your lives haven't overlapped for so long that you struggle to find common reference points. They were, however, now both half-making an effort to reconnect.

Calum went up the steps, rang the doorbell and waited. The light was on and music was playing. It sounded like Meatloaf.

He rang the bell again. Suddenly the door swung open and there stood Peter Pan. Or was it Robin Hood?

'Yes?' he said, sounding at once both defensive and threatening.

'Is Alastair in?'

'Nope, he's gone to Australia.'

'Australia?'

'Yep. Two weeks ago. I'm house-sitting while he's away.'

He had a weird accent that he couldn't place.

'Oh, right. How long's he gone for?'

'Three months maybe. Depends how it pans out.'

'Have you got an address or anything for him over there? I'm an old friend of his.'

'Hang on a sec. I'll go and get it.'

Calum couldn't put his finger on what accent he had. He watched him walk back along the hall. He had the bouncy gait of those people whose heels barely touch the ground when they walk.

There was no sign of a bow or quiver. It seemed natural for Calum not to question the outfit as its wearer gave the impression that no explanation was necessary.

He returned with a pen and paper and handed them to Calum.

'Here you go. He's travelling around, but his base address at his cousin's is:

9 Anna Ave, Paddington, Sydney, Australia. Don't know the postcode but I'm sure it'll get there.'

'Have you got a new phone number for him? I've been trying to text and phone but the number doesn't seem to work anymore.'

'Nah, he's probably gone phoneless while he's out there or something.'

'Cheers anyway. I'm Calum, by the way. You off to a fancy dress party?'

'No.'

'Right, OK. Thanks a lot. See you.'

As he turned and walked away down the path in bemusement, he looked at the address again.

9 Anna Avenue

Anna. Anna Aharoni. Something of a coincidence. What was going on? Somebody was definitely toying with him. He felt like a character in a book. A marionette. Maybe it was just a coincidence? Or a sign that fate had crossed his path with Anna Aharoni's for a reason?

He still needed to do something about the purse when he got home. Imagine she'd gone missing or something and he'd still got her purse? How would that look?

Passing his car as he reached home, he noticed a flyer on the windscreen. He lifted it out from under the wiper and turned it round so he could read it. It was slightly damp from the drizzle that had started to fall. In large bold Times New Roman it said:

Alere Flammam Veritatis

His secondary school motto. *Let the flame of truth shine.*

He was definitely being sent a message. Should he be worried or was someone just winding him up?

He looked around to see if his reaction was being observed. Nothing untoward. It must be Ally, but why, and why now?

He rolled the 'flyer' up, put it into his coat pocket and headed into the flat.

6

Recumbent in the bathtub, Maria Cormack was listening to chill-out jazz on the radio. A deflated octopus of discarded black tights lay on the wooden stool next to her.

She had lit some candles at the foot of the bath and the shadow cast by the washbasin resembled Brendan Behan in profile. She often saw faces in patterns and shapes. Most mornings when she brushed her teeth, she would look for the moustachioed Viking's head that was discernible in the frosted bathroom windowpane, if you tilted your head at a certain angle.

The music was lovely. Richly layered, textured, deep and somehow both dark and light, it was music she'd always subconsciously longed to hear but had never come across until now. She didn't even care about finding out who it was by; she just wanted to let it flow through and around her and sink a little deeper into the water. Surveying the cluster of stars through the skylight, she felt the urge to float up and lick them all to feel them fizz on her tongue. She hadn't felt this good for ages.

Sublime. *Sublime*. It was a curious word; how it somehow managed to overcome the negative connotations of its constituent parts. The demeaning prefix 'sub' juxtaposed with 'lime' somehow conjuring up limescale or quicklime rather than the fruit. Maybe it was because there was also 'slime' in there too and the word, as a whole, looked like it could mean something like 'septic'.

In that respect, it was similar to *pulchritude*, which looked ugly, but actually meant beauty. Or *coruscating*, which also has the opposite meaning to what you'd expect.

There was a lot of pressure on writers to know the meanings of words and be able to pronounce them correctly, especially on a peer-to-peer basis. She must have looked up the word *sanguine* at least a half a dozen times since first encountering it in a Thomas Hardy poem she did for her English Literature GCSE. She'd also needed to check the pronunciation of *hegemony* on a similar number of occasions. Some things just didn't stick, but she was tireless about looking things up. There was still a lot of snobbery in some literary circles and you had to work extra hard not to put a foot wrong if you had been brought up in her environment. So much more had to be learned if you had grown up in a non-RP environment. There was a lot of catching up to do, which she'd done by reading a ridiculous amount, but you weren't always sure how to pronounce some words that you came across and therefore avoided using them in certain circles.

Sublime. She could feel the two sides of the word struggling with each other for supremacy. She said the word out loud again. *Sublime.* It sounded better than it looked. Maybe it was something to do with the stress being on the second syllable, lending it a continental feel? She pronounced it the French way and was tempted to think that it sounded more attractive in English. She wasn't sure. It was a toss-up.

She repeated the word several times to the rhythm of the music, stretching out the final syllable and letting it wash over her like a mantra.

It was curious how sublime moments often came to her when she was alone. She wondered if it was because she was better able to focus and engage with an experience, absorb it and let it roll through her without the distraction of others?

She was beginning to get fed up with being alone, though. She would always need her space—and not only when she was writing—but she was definitely starting to feel that her sabbatical from relationships might be drawing to a close. She had always assumed that she'd have children at some point but recently she'd started to feel that the aureate sands of future family holidays might be slipping through her fingers. Her sister had never intended not to have kids, but by the time she'd met the right person, it was too late. The desperate repeated bouts of IVF were in vain.

Fate, however, in the shape of Circle line roulette, may be coming to her aid by throwing up someone from her past. Someone she'd had a mad, secret crush on at school.

She exhaled a wry 'huh' through her nose as she recollected the serendipitous nature of the encounter and then immediately wondered what the name of the verb for that gentle exclamation was. A wordsmith was expected to know this kind of thing. Was there even a word for it? Some languages were bound to have one.

She hadn't been one hundred per cent sure it was him (though the accent more or less fitted) until she'd trailed him half way round London to his flat and then checked the electoral roll and phone directory. Bullseye!

His hair was now receding, but she didn't mind that, and the same intense look in the eyes was still there. She'd felt him look at her a couple of times, but had the feeling he hadn't recognized her. Why would he?

He wasn't wearing a wedding ring and seemed to be dropping the kids off at their mum's. Cute kids.

Negligible online presence—to his credit. This was, hopefully, going to be good—very good. She couldn't believe her eyes—well she could; things had often seemed to play into her hands since she'd moved to London. She'd almost started to believe that she had a magical quality.

She had looked him up a couple of times over the years, but had never found anything of consequence. She had always wondered what had become of him and had imagined all manner of exotic things. Predictably, the reality was rather banal.

He must have been living down here quite a while. What does he do for a living?

He didn't look *un*well-off. *Teaching, I bet. Chances are...* He looked a bit teacherly in his navy-blue chinos. She would soon find out.

She slid her body down and sank further under the water, totally immersing her head for a couple of seconds in the underbeing.

10

Originating in the asteroid belt between Mars and Jupiter and orbiting the Sun at an average distance of 425 million km, an unnamed meteoroid 6.6m in diameter, created by the collision of two asteroids travelling at one thousand mph, is nearing the end of a one-hundred-thousand-year odyssey as it heads randomly towards the Earth's atmosphere.

Reaching a speed of around forty-five thousand mph, it enters the mesosphere at an altitude of eighty-five km and an angle of forty-five degrees, where the atmospheric pressure heats it so that it glows and creates a shining trail of orange/yellow gases and melted particles (faintly visible in the northern European dusk), which turn it into a meteor or 'shooting star'.

While still several miles up, the main surviving piece of this meteoroid (now roughly the size of a cricket ball and classified as a meteorite) reaches terminal velocity of between two hundred and four hundred miles per hour. Falling, falling, falling, still falling.

A little over a minute later, this meteorite of the type chondrite and mainly formed of bronzite, olivine, pyroxene, plagioclase, metals and sulphides plummets noiselessly through the still, cooling, crepuscular bankside air above the River Lee, passing less than six feet in front of the poised beak and inscrutable gaze of an unnamed kingfisher (let's call him Julian) and lands with a deeply satisfying hiss and sonorous plop in the darkening autumn water just below his perch. A single drop of splashed river water lands on his head and sits there quivering almost imperceptibly, offering a brief micro-panoramic reflected view of the surrounding scene in the gathering gloom.

The smooth, jet-black rock with a granitey, black pudding-like interior hits the river bed, scattering a shoal of minnows and creates a small, reverberating crater before rolling a few feet downstream and settling itself in amongst the shingle and sediment.

15

Tuesday

The following morning, Calum Roche awoke at 7.07am. It was a shaving day, so he splashed his face with water as hot as he could get it from the tap and then, looking up at himself in the bathroom mirror, noticed a micro-pustule in the crease at the side of his left nostril. Although he knew it wasn't quite ready for squeezing, it was clear that he couldn't go to work with it as it was, as it would inevitably ripen and grow over the morning. So he dug both index finger nails into the tight flesh either side of it until his eyes started to water and the zit exploded like a tiny custard pie onto the reflection of his face in the mirror.

Sometimes he'd gone into work and not noticed he'd had one until mid-morning. He would try to console himself with the thought that his colleagues, rather than being disgusted by the zit and his lack of awareness of it, did, in fact, admire the lack of vanity that obviously not examining himself closely in the mirror before leaving the house implied.

As he stood behind her, brushing her hair, Molly had once told him that he didn't look as good in the mirror as he did in real life, but knowing her, it could be one of her precocious little wind-ups.

It had also recently occurred to him that he could be suffering from some form of body dysmorphia and that his physique in general might actually look a lot better than he thought it did. He had no idea really what kind of figure he cut in most people's eyes but surmised that it was vaguely unprepossessing.

Tubby or not tubby? That is the question…

He got on pretty well with the people at work, but didn't really know where he stood with most of them. He'd been there for almost ten years, teaching English as a foreign language, and had now more or less dropped the pretence that he was just filling in before moving on to a 'proper career'. Like many of his colleagues, he'd toyed with the idea of mainstream teaching, but Rachel's experiences there had convinced him that he wasn't cut out for that daily battle and although only seeing the girls at weekends meant that he had more time and energy to devote to his writing, he still hadn't properly been able to get down to it.

Unlike in a primary or secondary school, there was little sense of being part of the local community. You could try to kid yourself that you were part of the international community, but you were basically servicing the privileged, and the constant turnover of students made it feel transient, which just served to heighten his sense of anonymity.

When he wasn't at school, it was hard for him to actually picture himself standing up in front of a class, being the focus of attention and making an impression on the students. He generally felt so anonymous that he was always surprised when people that he hadn't met very often recognised and remembered him when they bumped into each other again.

Apart from when he was with the kids, and even sometimes then, he felt like a ghost. The ghostwriter of his own life? *His own spectre*.

Something that he needed to do was nagging away at the back of his mind. Why didn't he write things down? What day was it? Tuesday. The orange day. *Choozday.* It brought to mind some Italian kids coming out of a colleague's summer school class repeating the word in mock exaggeration of her drilling: *Chooozday, Chooozday, Chooozday!*

Going into the kitchen, he saw the purse on the table and put it into his work bag. He poured himself an orange juice, put the kettle on and got himself a bowl of Shreddies.

2

Anna Aharoni had had a bad few days. Last week, she'd somehow managed to open a door into her own face as she was going into a café, sustaining a cut just above the eyebrow. It had now started to scab up and was evolving into a mini strawberry fruit pastille. Then, a couple of days ago, she'd been walking along the street when an ordinary-looking guy walking ahead of her holding hands with his partner, suddenly, with no warning or build-up and without hardly even breaking his stride, expertly karate-kicked in the passenger window of a parked car and then carried on walking as though nothing had happened. The partner didn't even turn her head to look—it was as though he had merely coughed or sneezed. Anna was the only other person around and wasn't sure she hadn't imagined it until she passed the car and saw the shattered window. Why hadn't the alarm gone off? Her instinct would normally have been to shout out something like, 'Hey, what do you think you're doing?' Self-preservation, however, had kicked in and she really didn't know what to do now. She obviously felt she ought to do *something* but the guy was obviously dangerous. His partner was probably a nutter too. If she intervened, *he* might have qualms about attacking a woman, but the girlfriend probably wouldn't. The best thing was to report it. What could she have done anyway? She could hardly have performed a citizen's arrest. The other thing was that she was cutting it fine to get to her AA meeting on time. She also told herself that it was, after all, just damage to property and, what's more, it was some kind of fancy sports supercar; one of those ridiculous Ferraris or Lamborghinis or something. It just didn't sit well with her to do nothing, however, and she briefly considered the idea of nipping across the road and trying to briskly but discreetly get ahead of them and then double back towards them to secretly take photos of them with her camera phone. There was no point, though, it was too dark. All she could do was make a note of the time and hope that there was CCTV on the High Street that had captured them walking by at the time. She was really torn, because part of her wanted them to know that she had seen them, but on the other hand, was it worth the risk for what was just a relatively minor act of vandalism? The police almost certainly wouldn't think it was a big deal—nothing had been stolen and the owner obviously wasn't short of a bob or two. It would also be difficult to identify them from CCTV, however, as they were both wearing baseball caps. If she'd had time, she would definitely have been tempted to follow them and would probably have had to make a superhuman effort not to. All she could do, in the end , was just focus on the fact that the owner of the car was probably a wanker and had no doubt done numerous despicable things that had gone unpunished

Who knows, it may well have been a targeted attack rather than the gratuitous, spontaneous act that it seemed to be.

She contacted the police the following day to give all the details, even though she knew she was almost certainly wasting her time and nothing would come of it.

Later that same day, she lost her purse. She didn't think there had been much money in it—maybe a tenner and some change, but it was still a pain. Her Oyster card was in it too.

She'd cancelled the cards and fortunately, no money had gone out of her account. It was just annoying, and she loved that purse. It was made of raspberry-red, Moroccan leather with the symbol of the goddess Isis on it, and was ingeniously designed so that she could fit everything in it and still be able to slip it comfortably into her jeans pocket. The main reason she was desperate to get it back, though, was that her older brother Ben had bought it for her not long before he'd died while on a training exercise with the Fleet Air Arm.

He'd been in a helicopter flying over the sea in Devon when he'd somehow fallen out of the open side door and plunged to his death. In her eyes, the inquest never satisfactorily explained why the door was left open or why, as a fairly experienced officer, he hadn't been wearing a harness at the time. He might have survived if he'd landed directly in the sea, but he caught the side of a tiny rocky island before hitting the water.

She'd never got over it and couldn't help suspecting that there might have been some foul play involved. She often had nightmares where she was the one falling out of the helicopter, passing the point of no return and experiencing that awful moment of realisation that you are doomed—that you were falling to your death.

A void of darkness had opened up that could never fully be filled. Alcohol could temporarily numb the pain, but ultimately only made things worse, and extreme immersion in her work only served as a distraction for brief periods. The birth and care of her son, Noah, was the only thing that offered any real respite, but even now, from time to time, she would inevitably get that sickening chill feeling of dread and loss.

It would be his forty-first birthday on Friday and she'd be making her way back to the common and the tree they'd planted in his name. Her mum and dad and Dan would be there and there'd be a pub lunch in the Fleece, where she'd burn to have a drink to toast his beautiful head and quell the singing hollowness in her veins.

The purse was one of her most treasured possessions and she felt so guilty and foolish for having lost it. The funny thing was she'd seen one of her favourite writers on the Tube around the time she must have last had it. The writer had even responded to her discreet smile and subtle nod of acknowledgement with a little benign smile of her own. Perhaps she had recognised her too and admired her work?

That could have been the precise moment she was pickpocketed. Presuming she was pickpocketed… She'd been pickpocketed on her sole trip to Barcelona and it wasn't a nice feeling. She'd felt violated by the city at large.

She must have had it when she got on the Tube, as she'd still had her Oyster card then, but they'd let everyone through the big gate at the other end because the automatic gates weren't working. She didn't realise that she didn't have it with her until she called in at the local shop for a jar of capers.

Gavin's phone number was in there as well, written on the back of a receipt. She stupidly hadn't got round to putting it into the contacts on her mobile.

She didn't hold out much hope of it turning up at lost property, but she'd try them later—you probably had to wait at least twenty-four hours anyway for something to find its way back there.

She decided to go out for a walk before getting down to some work—she always liked to get out in the fresh air and get the blood circulating as soon after breakfast as possible. Dark clouds could easily settle in and suffuse her mind if she failed to do so.

When she got onto the high street, she saw the homeless young woman again that she'd seen outside Tesco's for the first time the evening before. She was crouched, head down, in the morning cold with a thin, khaki, army surplus jacket covering her whole body like a poncho with arms. At first glance, it made it look as if she was a double leg amputee. Her pallid face had a taut, hunted look. Still several paces away, Anna made up her mind to put some money in the poor woman's cup and as she approached, a voice was invoking her to stop and chat and find out where she would be sleeping that night.

Why don't you stop? Why aren't you stopping? Why don't you give her some real help? Invest some time and care. She stooped to drop the coins in the cup, half-hesitated and walked on. The self-recrimination she felt at her failure to stop increased as it occurred to her that the poor woman might be wearing a thin coat deliberately in order to gain more sympathy, and was exacerbated by the familiar acknowledgement that these genuine feelings of compassion and compunction would most likely once again have faded away in a matter of minutes. For now, though, the girl's hollow, drug-haunted skull of a face was seared on her mind. She wanted to do something, but what could she realistically do? She wasn't going to give her her sofa for the night.

A little further on as she passed the new cafe, she noticed that they'd started selling Portuguese tarts. She joined the small queue and bought one to have with her flat white.

17

While Calum was on his most convoluted route to work, he felt like he was being followed. He'd *thought* about the possibility of being followed or someone lying in wait for him before, but never *felt* it. He'd stopped a few times to look in shop windows and have a casual look round, but saw no one untoward. The phone message and the purse were also dominating his thoughts. He'd played the message again that morning and was pretty certain he'd detected a slight northern accent. If the number *was* a code, the simplest one would be that each number represented a letter of the alphabet.

If you took away the 020, it gave you CAIRAM, which didn't mean anything to him.

All a Google search had yielded was that it meant, 'They fell' in Portuguese.

They fell.

Soldiers in the Great War fell.

Horses fall at hurdles.

He, himself, had fallen in a way. And Alastair too.

The other kids at school as well, perhaps.

Or maybe that wasn't the code, or it wasn't even a code at all?

It had got IRA in there. C A IRA M. Calling all IRA members? It couldn't be that. That was ridiculous.

He suddenly became aware of his surroundings as a bus travelling too fast and too close to the kerb swept past. He stared after the bus for a few moments with a bleak feeling in his soul.

He felt exposed around his neck and ears without a hat or a scarf. It was definitely starting to feel autumnal.

3

As soon as he finished work, Calum headed off to get a jiffy bag and post the purse. As he turned out of the school gateposts, he noticed a missing cat sign pinned onto the plane tree rooted to the pavement in front.

A suspicious number of cats seemed to go missing in that neighbourhood, but this one caught his eye as the picture showed the cat wearing sunglasses and a Stone Roses T-shirt. Taking a closer look, he saw that the cat's name was Bede. The contact number also looked familiar. He rummaged for the piece of paper that he'd written the answerphone number on and saw that it was the same one.

St Bede's was the name of his old secondary school and he used to have a Stone Roses shirt very similar to that.

Someone was definitely messing around with him. The obvious suspect was Ally, and though the voice on the phone was female, he could easily have got someone else to call. Maybe he wasn't even in Australia either? On the other hand, he really couldn't imagine him going to all this trouble and what would be the point?

It suddenly struck him that there might be a more sinister angle to it all—someone down here in London might be letting him know that they were au fait with his past. He wondered if he should take the poster down and, deciding that it would look suspicious to be seen looking round to see if anyone was coming, he opted for decisive insouciance and casually tore it down. He was putting it into his pocket when a colleague, Tom, appeared at this side.

'Been found then, has it?'

'Er, yeah. The cat's a friend of mine's who lives round the corner. It turned up last night in a neighbour's shed.'

'That's good. Moggies always seem to be going missing round here. Fancy a pint?'

'No, I need to go and get something in the post.'

'Catch you later then.'

'Yep.'

Sometimes it was easier to lie to save time. The annoying thing for Calum, though, was that he often felt as if he was lying when he was telling the truth. This air of guilt, however, also served to make whoever he was talking to think he was indeed lying.

This involuntary self-incrimination also manifested itself whenever he entered a shop on his own. Often, he would have to remind himself that he hadn't stolen anything and had no intention of doing so as yet another store detective overtly tracked him along the aisles. Once, he'd even been followed out of a small health food shop by an assistant and an alerted colleague after an innocent request for a not- too-obscure herbal remedy and a spot of browsing. He would make the perfect decoy for an actual shoplifter.

The ironic thing was that when he had actually been a prolific shoplifter in his teens, he had never been caught. The elated feeling of being completely in the clear when he decided to give it up a few months into his first year at university was still tangible. He'd quit while he was ahead and got away with it.

He must have looked more innocent then and maybe the legacy of those criminal pursuits was belatedly manifesting itself in his features, giving him a guilty, shifty look.

It was the same story when he went through customs. He nearly always felt, and therefore looked, guilty even though he knew he had nothing untoward in his possession. Once on the way back from France to Dover on the ferry, he'd been strip-searched and had all his belongings meticulously examined, until, unable to find anything at all illicit, the customs officers were reluctantly forced to send him on his way.

The sudden cry of a gull snapped him out of this reverie as he approached the post office. No sign of a seabird, but he could see the moon up above. The bone-faced moon. Not quite so bone-faced in the daytime. A smoky, wafer-like, projected image; it was hard to believe that it was three-dimensional. Insubstantial. Smelling of gunpowder.

He posted the purse with a mixture of unease and relief. He wasn't sure where the unease was coming from—all he was trying to do was help. Maybe he should just have taken it round in person, but then it looks like you're expecting a reward. He'd done that once as a kid, traipsing to the next town only for guy to rummage around in his pocket for change to give him. He should have guessed that the guy wouldn't have any notes to give him as they would have been in the wallet.

The change he'd left inside the purse wouldn't rattle around as he'd sellotaped it all together in a little plastic bag. He'd also taped all round the jiffy bag to completely seal it up.

He was just trying to help. He liked helping people. What do teachers do if not help people? Strangely, he'd never thought of it in those simple terms before and it made him feel good. Was it a revelation or just something he'd forgotten? He straightened his back, walked a little taller and breathed a bit more deeply as he sometimes reminded himself to do, sneaking a glance in a car window to make sure that he wasn't overly sergeant-major erect.

He strode a little faster and started to feel slightly light-headed, but in a good way. He gathered pace and the feeling started to become almost euphoric. It was almost as if someone had slipped something into his tea, but it felt natural; as if his hormones and the chemicals in his brain had somehow aligned to create a sense of complete metabolic well-being, mental sharpness and goodwill.

He felt loose and fluid and energetic—like Muhammad Ali—floating like a butterfly and stinging like a bee.

That was when the idea came to him. The idea of becoming a kind of guardian angel. He would choose random strangers and secretly help them; do them little clandestine favours. He could do it and then write about his experiences.

He looked around to see if there was any sort of a confirmatory positive sign or omen in the shop or street names, but nothing stood out. This minor disappointment was soon dissolved by the overriding sense of excitement, however. This could be it—the big idea that he'd been waiting for…The writing was on the wall. He hadn't felt this positive or optimistic for a long, long time.

He was all too aware that he had an ingrained tendency to focus on the negative. It was one of the major factors in Rachel's gradual disillusionment with him. If he looked at any painting, his eye would go straight to the flaw and not be able to overlook it. The same with the flaws in her friends, and even his own friends' characters.

Even as he had been approaching Euston through the looming, drab, sprawling suburbs on one of his first lone adult trips to London, he couldn't help thinking about all the stabbings, beatings, rapes and thefts that were going on across the city at that very moment. It wasn't that he overlooked the positive side—London was the one true powerhouse left in the country and one of the few places where there was a buzz in the air or any genuine international glamour, but behind the scenes he couldn't help imagining Hieronymus Bosch's Garden of Earthly Delights and it made him think how much easier it seemed to be to do harm than good in life. It was almost as if harm was a gravitational force that some people couldn't help but succumb to.

Hardly anyone, who wasn't under the influence of ecstasy or something, went up to strangers to give them a hug or compliment, but people were robbed, abused and assaulted by strangers all the time.

You'd think that for every negative, there'd be a positive to maintain the equilibrium. Maybe there was—there was all the charity work that went on, of course, but maybe there was also a network of people surreptitiously going around doing good deeds… If he did that and then wrote about it, he could redress another bias towards the negative he perceived in society.

It was so easy to create fictional horror, to dream up gruesome acts of violence and macabre scenarios. You just had to look around you for inspiration. Every kitchen in the land housed an innocent assortment of gruesome instruments of death or torture.

Take the humble cheese grater. It was easy to imagine a scene in an East End gangster movie where a hapless minor hoodlum is being tortured by having the skin grated off different parts of his body; his shoulder, feet, cheeks, etc.

'*Let's see just how cheesy this smart aleck really is and we'll have some nice Parmesan for our spag bol this evening into the bargain. It might be a tad on the mature side... We had "grate" expectations of you, my friend. This is all rather disappointing. Very disappointing.*'

It would be interesting to analyse what proportion of fiction dealt with crime.

A brief mental scan through Shakespeare suggested it was pretty high.

His story would attempt to have all the edge and suspense of noir, but the key acts would be acts of anonymous altruism and benevolence rather than violence and death.

Previous experience had taught him, however, that coming up with the general concept and making notes here and there was the easy part of writing and that the onset of the execution stage would, in all probability, plunge him into frustration and disillusionment. He had, therefore, hitherto mainly succumbed to the temptation of postponing the execution for as long as possible, to preserve the glowing potential of the original idea.

This time, however, he was determined to approach it differently—in manageable chunks. Possibly a series of interwoven short stories with an overarching storyline narrated from different angles.

It would be nice to feel that he was building a sense of excitement for once as he was writing, rather than dissipating it, and to be able to rekindle the feeling of quiet, absorbed exhilaration that he used to get when a drawing or painting was shaping up to be good and he'd felt as if he was really capturing something.

He'd written a few poems that he was quite pleased with, but had found prose to be a very different kettle of fish altogether. Writing a great novel, it seemed to him, must be the pinnacle of artistic achievement.

So, who would be the first beneficiary of this scheme? It would be funny to turn the tables on whoever was behind the phone message, flyer and cat poster. It must be someone from his past and it simply *had* to be linked with the purse too. He'd have another look at that number tonight and see if he could come up with anything else. He could ask his brother, who was a maths teacher, to look at it, but he'd probably think he was losing his marbles.

CAIRAM. They fell.

There might be more messages too. He might even be being followed right now. He turned to cross the street and had a good look around in both directions. If he found out who it was, he could start following them. Two people trying to tail each other…

He'd be interested to see how that would pan out.

19

Wednesday

Maria Cormack left the house to the sound of morning gulls, wondering how they managed to be both an uplifting cry of freedom and like a novice fiddler scraping sounds out of a violin.

'It is I, seagull.'

She'd listened to a programme about Valentina Tereshkova, the first woman in space, the night before and 'seagull' was the call name that the pioneering cosmonaut had radioed down to earth with after the launch. It sounded like a feminist rallying cry.

One of the episodes that had stayed with Maria was that on the way to the launch pad, the cosmonauts had the ritual of stopping to pee on the tyre of the bus taking them there. It was some kind of tribute to Yuri Gagarin, apparently. The phone rang at that point, so she never got to find out why.

'I am seagull, I am seagull!'

Maybe it was a nostalgic yearning for the seaside of our childhood that made it sound uplifting.

She felt the urge to whistle. Was it acceptable in public? She couldn't recall if she'd ever seen anyone whistling as they sauntered along the street. Perhaps it was only jaunty, sauntering men in old black and white films who did it.

She'd dreamt about Calum last night—it was strange how sometimes dreams could seem more vivid than reality. Just for a while—the feeling quickly fades.

They were back at school in Mrs. Mulligan's English class. St Bede's looked different but *felt* like the same place. They were going through the opening scene in *Anthony and Cleopatra* and Calum was reading aloud the part of Cleopatra and she the part of Anthony. Wondering why the roles were that way round, she grew increasingly frustrated by the proceedings and as the sniggering of the rest of the class turned into open laughter that even Mrs. Mulligan joined in with, she woke up suddenly.

She and Calum had been in the same class for a few subjects, but she suspected that he was only vaguely aware of her existence. Although she'd generally been careful not to give any indication that she was interested in him, she had on one occasion casually hung around in the park near his house and feebly tried to bond with his little brother in the hope that positive feedback would get back to Calum.

She knew now that being aware that someone is interested in you can very often arouse your interest in them in turn and make you look more favourably upon them, but back then she wasn't confident enough to stick her neck out.

She always tried to make sure that she sat somewhere behind him in class, preferably slightly to the side so she could observe him undetected.

Maybe it was the fact that he was a bit odd himself that gave her the faintest hope that she stood a chance with him.

She liked odd. She'd always preferred odd numbers to even, even though they felt kind of unlucky.

Even numbers were like the goody-goodies, the straightforward, archetypal heroes, whereas odd numbers were like the anti-heroes, the underdogs, the rebels.

Being left-handed felt the same too. Sinister? I don't think so!

For the same reason, she had always preferred tails over heads—it felt like odd versus even. Odd numbers were like the minor chords and even numbers the major.

Some months even had an odd feel to them—February, March, September, October, November. Oddly, they weren't evenly—or even oddly, for that matter—spaced throughout the year. They just had a dark, mysterious, minor chord feel to them.

The same principle couldn't be applied to the days of the week though. Wednesday did have an odd feel to it, but that was probably just down to Wednesday's child being 'full of woe'.

Her thing with the days of the week was synesthesia. Wednesday was green for her. Her nana always said that green was unlucky—she never bet on jockeys wearing green—pink was the lucky colour. Piggott in pink was a guaranteed winner. None of the days of the week were pink for her, though. Thursday was purple, Friday brown, Saturday black (strangely), Sunday white and yellow, like the Vatican flag. The colour for Monday didn't come through very clearly, but she had a vague sense that it was a very dark blue, the darkest possible blue, but the impression wasn't anywhere near as sharp as the others. Tuesday was an orangey red.

Why didn't weeks have names like days and months do? Maybe they did in some cultures… Maybe she should come up with some names for them herself in a future fantasy novel. Fifty-two names taken from all the continents, maybe linked with events or festivals that often take place during that week in particular places. She could sneak in some references to family members and personal heroes too. Alternatively, they could all just be made up names placed in alphabetical order twice—that would fit very neatly indeed. Maybe it would even catch on in certain quarters, initially as a cult, but eventually growing to such an extent that weeks would come to eclipse months and someone's birthday might be written as 4/48/2024.

What would be seen as the first day of the week though? Most westerners believe it's Monday of course, but her time in Portugal had taught her that the Portuguese word for Saturday was *Sabado,* which referred to the Sabbath, the seventh day of the week. She later discovered that it was the same in Spanish, which made her wonder why it wasn't the word for Sunday, which she had always been led to believe was the Sabbath—the day of rest. She looked into it and it seemed pretty clear that, according to the Bible, Saturday was the Sabbath, as was still the case in Judaism, and somewhere along the way it had been changed for Christians to Sunday.

So that would be her first decision. She was tempted to go with Sunday as the first day of the week, just to go against the grain, but you could also make a strong case for Saturday, as Friday was, after all, the end of the working week. Yes, maybe she'd have Saturday as day one. It was the best day after all.

She wondered what day Calum was born on. She remembered that his birthday was in May but she couldn't remember which day—the 29th or 31st? Was he Thursday's child like her with *far to go*? The only ambiguous one. All of the other days were unambiguously positive except for poor old Wednesday's child. It was all a load of old crap of course, but the ambivalence of Thursday's child would be fitting for him.

In her experience, most men could be divided into three basic categories: knobs, yobs or slobs, or a combination thereof.

Calum had definitely had something of the knob and yob in him, but that was pretty much standard in teenage boys. He'd got into the odd fight and dicked around with his mates, but there was a sensitive, vulnerable and intelligent side that was at odds with the knob and yob. He was a bit quirky too and the knob, yob, slob thing didn't cover that.

He hadn't been much to look at, really, if she tried to view him objectively. He'd had spots and short legs. He'd actually looked taller than she'd remembered him sitting there on the Tube, but when he'd stood up to get off she'd realized that he was just tall sitting down.

She was intrigued by the gender reversal in the dream.

'I'll set a bourn how far to be beloved.'
'Then must thou needs find out new heaven, new earth.'

He'd read his lines in what seemed to be an intentionally wooden and uncomfortable way and she'd felt angry and frustrated with the teacher for giving them the wrong roles. It would have been more appropriate if it had been a role reversal between Pip and Estella in *Great Expectations,* as they'd done that book too.

She wasn't entirely sure whether the dream was a sign that she should pursue the course that she was taking—certainly not on the face of it, as it was a doomed affair, but she had felt a strong sense of complicity between them in the dream, despite the gender shift and Calum's affected lack of commitment. She'd also dreamt that she could fly again. She'd had that dream so many times now that she almost believed she could actually fly in real life if she could just put her mind to it and be able to replicate the feeling she had in the dreams. It just seemed so easy and natural. It was almost an everyday thing when it happened in the dreams—exhilarating and enjoyable, yes, but definitely doable, like, say, ice-skating or horse riding very well. Certainly not anything supernatural.

She was wrenched out of her reverie by the sight of a man dressed as Peter Pan walking towards her. It very much looked like the same guy she'd seen on the Tube a few days before, whom she had assumed was on his way to a fancy dress party, even though he had seemed incongruously sombre in his demeanour. She obviously didn't want to stare at him as he approached—it was unwise for a woman to make eye contact with a male stranger at the best of times, let alone one who obviously had some issues, but she had an uncanny ability to take things in out of the corner of her eye without focusing on them directly. His burly build was at odds with the character he was portraying and the tunic he wore was so short it revealed an expanse of long powerful thigh that she found at the same time both comical and sensual. He obviously saw it as a shorts day. As they passed, she couldn't help glancing at him while they were adjacent to each other for a second and was convinced it was the same person. He had the greenest eyes she'd ever seen. Kelly green. It was hard to be sure that they weren't lenses, but she didn't think so. She instinctively turned round to look at him a second later and over his shoulder he said,

'Tis an odd bird the fish.'

Smiling, she watched his red-feathered alpine hat receding through the throng.

A meaningless coincidence? No doubt the book she was working on increased the chances of such encounters, as it was based on people she randomly came across on her day-to-day travels. She'd written down the names of all the stations on the Circle line in the correct order in a circle on a large piece of paper placed on an old fold-up card table she'd got from a charity shop, and every week or so she would place a pen in the centre and spin it. Whichever stop the nib of the pen pointed to was the appointed station for that journey and whoever was the first person to board her carriage via the nearest door would be the chosen one—her Circle line roulette marionette— and the beneficiary of a kindness or the recipient of a piece of harmless mischief.

The project was still very much in the embryonic stage and could well evolve into something completely different along the way. So far, there had just been one round proper of Circle line roulette and the first person to benefit from the spin of her pen was a tall, shy-looking woman. On two occasions, Maria had played the role of the artful dodger in reverse by first surreptitiously placing a note saying, '*You are wonderful*' in her coat pocket and then slipping some beautiful seashells into her tote bag.

She had been torn about whether to make the treats one-offs or not as she was, of course, worried that the chosen ones might feel stalked and freak out about multiple gifts. She therefore had some business cards made up that said:

You have been selected by the Kindness Institute to receive a few little treats. Don't be freaked out, just enjoy them and pass the positivity on!

And she'd slipped them into both envelopes. She was also aware that the randomly selected recipient might be completely undeserving of her charity. However, as a determinist, she held the view that ultimately everything in life was down to luck and she would therefore tailor her gifts or mischief to whoever the wheel of fortune presented to her, based on whatever inclinations she developed after observing them for a while. The selection was random but the response was selective and designed to offset in some small way the poor hand that some people had been dealt.

She fully accepted that her success as a writer was entirely due to factors beyond her control; she hadn't willed herself to be articulate and imaginative, to have a good memory or the character that enabled her to dedicate herself to a solitary task for months on end. She'd also had no control over whether one of the agents that she'd sent her first novel to would like it and be able to persuade a major publisher to take her on.

Life had always struck her as win-win or lose-lose. There were, in the main, vicious cycles for the poor or weak and virtuous cycles for the wealthy or powerful. It was an upside-down world, where the rich and famous were showered with free gifts and services they scarcely needed and could easily afford to buy while the disadvantaged or marginalised were hounded and victimised for simply trying to survive.

In her scheme, however, the wealthy and other people that she didn't morally approve of wouldn't be penalised or punished. The mischief in those cases would instead be designed to gently encourage the correction of a flaw in their character or behaviour. She would only possibly act as a vengeful god in the fictional representation of events.

That was the concept anyway, but she knew that it could all very well change as it went along—that it could head off at a tangent that she shouldn't ignore or resist; a tangent she should embrace.

Calum was a case in point. He hadn't actually been the chosen one that day; he'd got on at the station before the designated one and she was so taken up with working out whether it was definitely him or not that she almost forgot to pay attention to who had actually got on first at Moorgate.

This, of course, raised the question of who had been offered up more randomly —the person produced by the Circle line roulette system or the one thrown up by pure fate or coincidence?

Since reading about the philosophical concept of *disponibilité* at university, she'd always aspired to be more available and open to events. Going with the flow seemed to be the key to living life to the full, but, of course, the practicalities of life dictated that most people could only really do this during periods when they weren't working or bringing up children. It was different for professional writers, however. She had the flexibility to be '*disponible*'.

With her interest in chance encounters and *objets trouvés*, she'd also wanted to find out who the lovely-looking purse belonged to, but Calum had got to it first. He was the greater prize though; the purse just made the encounter more interesting.

If people knew what she was up to…When the book came out, everyone would assume that it was pure fiction or loosely based on an acquaintance, but if only they knew the petty lengths that she had gone to—the subterfuge, game-playing and sneaking around that had gone into it.

Even if it did come out, however, how would people know that it was actually true?

The truth was always ultimately subjective, and even if she admitted it, some people were bound to think that she was just playing her usual games around the blurred lines between fact and fiction.

Sneaking around wasn't that outlandish for a writer anyway, and although she did occasionally get recognized—that attractive woman in the headscarf on the Tube who had smiled and nodded obviously knew who she was—it wasn't as if she was a household name.

Graham Greene once said that being a writer was very much like being a spy—you quietly observe people, make notes and gather material—you even secretly record them sometimes. You try to get to the truth, or at least a credible representation of the truth. That's why, with a few notable exceptions, most writers tended to be introverts. It was pretty hard to carefully observe others if you were the life and soul of the party, regaling your coterie with witty anecdotes. You generally needed to be unobtrusive and unassuming. Greene, with his apologetic stoop, didn't buck that trend.

As she slipped past Waterstones, she noticed that they'd taken her book out of the window. The bastards.

Part of her was surprised and disappointed that Calum almost certainly hadn't recognised her. You'd think that coming from the same small town, he would have heard about her success and made the connection. Maybe he just wasn't aware of it and hadn't seen a recent picture of her. She did look very different now.

You could usually tell if someone recognizes you… It had been strange to discern a flicker of attraction in his eyes. It had made her feel like someone else—to him she *was* someone else.

It took her back to all those years at school feeling overlooked. Back then, she'd hoped she was like one of the clover flowers that her granddad had pointed out to her on one of their Sunday evening walks—outshone by the daisies and buttercups, but appreciated by the rare few.

Although she knew that people now often found her attractive, she still felt like a clover, but now more the red than the unassuming white. *Trifolium pratense.* Her grandad seemed to know the names of most of the flowers and stars. She remembered what he used to say to her:

> *Look up, look up, look all around.*
> *Pick your eyes up off the ground.*
> *You'll be amazed what can be found*
> *by the chimneys, in the clouds.*

She wasn't sure where he'd got it from and she also knew he'd liked to look at stuff on the ground as much as in the air, but it was something that she often reminded herself to do—especially in London, where she often felt so hemmed in.

Accordingly, she looked up at the sky. It was a fresh pale blue, dappled with very white, visibly drifting, clouds—all very vivid and alive like the sky in the Monet painting of a woman with a parasol that she'd rather uncoolly had on her wall at uni. The one where a young woman in a long white dress is viewed from below as she stands on the brow of a hill, and you can almost feel the breeze and sense the movement of the clouds behind her.

Seemingly ordinary skies could be casually amazing—a shifting, ephemeral, panoramic tableau displayed for our diurnal delectation. Who needed the Northern Lights?

His kids were really sweet. Beautiful hair—the perfect shade of red. She wondered if they were the sort to look up and around and notice things. Or did they have their heads buried in books the whole time? Good choices of books, though. Potential future Cormack readers?

She had been trying to work out what their mum looked like by comparing their faces with Calum's and subtracting the difference. She hadn't seen him for over twenty years, since he'd been expelled from school. She'd once put a speculative message on Friends Reunited simply saying, '*Hello Calum Roche*', but he'd never replied.

Nobody had known where he was or what he was up to, but she had stumbled across him and now knew where he lived and worked. She just needed to somehow engineer a meeting with him. The simplest way would be to just pretend to bump into him outside his school or something. A bit banal. She'd set the wheels in motion, but the question now, as ever for a writer, was how to proceed?

A large disapproving cloud had seemed to come from nowhere, obscuring the sun and she felt a few tibs of rain fall on her cheek and nose.

Having reached saturation point a couple of years previously, she hadn't trawled through any dating sites for a good old while. At the very least, the customary rogues gallery would be sure to raise a bit of a chuckle—the man in the Harry Potter outfit, the guy wearing a wedding ring, the one who had 'seriously considered a penis reduction', the other in a child's cycle helmet, the dude who ate his mate's cold sore scab for a fiver, the bloke who liked to be farted on, the fellow who was willing to admit that he'd not had sex with a man or boy, the man who only ate rice krispies and the various chaps who cunningly photographed themselves from just below normal hairline level down in order to conceal their baldness. God love them all.

Maybe she would take another little stroll down Lonely Avenue that evening and see whether any interesting new residents had arrived on the scene since the break up of a long-term relationship...

7

The sun was just setting behind the trees that lined her street as Anna's garden gate lurched open to let her through. Admiring the horse chestnut tree in next door's garden, she was struck by the sheer size of it—and the scale of trees in general.

They were the giants of the plant world, everyday wonders that were taken for granted. They were living botanical dinosaurs or the elephants of flora—their bark even resembled the skin of a pachyderm. Planted, grounded, earthed. She liked that—that's how she'd strived to feel since she'd stopped drinking.

There were slippery, soggy leaves everywhere. She didn't really like the autumn any more—its dampness, decay, dank and death, its rust and rot. She liked the words 'autumn' and 'autumnal', though, the shapes and connotations of the word —*Au* for gold—seemed to conjure up golden and orange leaves. A much less prosaic term than 'fall', though her natural contrariness often saw her challenging her compatriots' sneers about American English, by pointing out that many 'Americanisms' like 'fall' and 'trash' originated in the old country.

Her key slid easily into the lock and, as the door swung open, a smallish parcel addressed to her greeted her on the shelf in the communal hallway. She examined it for the telltale circle inside a square stamp telling her that it had been security cleared. Noah knew to leave any packages alone—she never needed to tell him anything twice, but she thought it better not to mention the marking so as not to risk tempting him into fiddling around looking for it.

This package was completely bound in sellotape like a mummified cellophane samosa, which would make it look rather suspicious if you didn't have an idea what the contents might be. To her, though, it looked and felt like it was the size and shape of her purse. It couldn't be… When she shook it there was no chinking of change, however. She went up to her flat, calling out, 'Hi, Noah?' as she entered.

'Hi Mum,' came the bright reply. He'd already texted to say he was home but it was still always a relief when she could see that he was actually there. He was very good at texting back promptly—he never kept her waiting for very long.

She went into the kitchen, got some scissors from the top drawer and carefully snipped at the bits of sellotape she could get at until she was able to unbandage the whole thing. There it was. It had only been a few days, but it still felt like she was seeing an old friend. Tears filled her eyes—she couldn't believe how relieved she was and she immediately thought of the last time she'd seen Ben before he died. He'd waved goodbye after her little birthday do and as he was bounding away down the garden path, he had done his usual trick of tripping himself up and stumbling for a few steps. Turning her head and leaning backwards slightly she called brightly through the kitchen doorway towards Noah's room.

'I've got my purse back.'

'Great!' came the reply.

Inside the purse there was a note, which read:

I found this on the Tube and got your address from the invoice inside. Hopefully, you haven't moved! I taped the change up so that it wouldn't give away what the contents were. Best wishes, Calum Roche.

No phone number, but if you put your number down, it's like you're looking to get a reward. He might be in the phone book. There couldn't be that many Calum Roches in London—presuming he did live in London. A glance at the postmark suggested he did.

Everything seemed to be there—no notes, but maybe there hadn't been a tenner in it after all. Noah's picture with the Zac Efron haircut was there—it was only a few years ago, but he'd changed quite a bit. The slip of paper with Gavin's number on was also there, so she put it into the contacts in her phone straight away. She looked at the now useless bank cards. It was still strange sometimes to see her real name in an official capacity.

After leaving university, she'd decided to use a professional pseudonym and had opted for Anna Heron—part of her felt a bit ashamed about it, but Anna Aharoni was a bit of a mouthful and she already had the surname Heron on her maternal grandmother's side anyway.

This had turned out to be a very wise move because the nature of the column she wrote for a national newspaper meant that she had received death threats and had had to take the precaution of never going to the office and of wearing a headscarf whenever she went out. She saw the irony in wearing a garment that usually attracted hostility in order to ward off danger, but as a journalist, she also viewed it as a kind of undercover experiment to experience how women perceived to be Muslim (or by the more discerning, Jewish) were treated in the current climate. One day, hopefully, when things had cooled down, she would be able to write an article about her experiences and maybe, eventually, even get a book out of it.

Although she'd never let on, she'd been secretly quite concerned when the threats started to appear—*as it only takes one nutter*—but eventually, as nothing had come of it, she had started to feel relatively safe and stopped being hyper-vigilant every time she walked down the street. She'd thought long and hard about what she'd say to Noah if he ever asked her why she wore headscarves outside, but, strangely, he never had. Fortunately, it had been winter when she first started wearing them and she normally wore the most modern-style tichel she could find. She was yet to come up with an entirely convincing explanation for it and he was bound to raise it one day soon. She could perhaps just say that she was getting in touch with her roots or offer a blithe, 'Every day just seems to be a bad hair day these days, I'm afraid, sunshine!' Perhaps he'd already guessed. He was pretty smart.

The old photo of her that the paper insisted accompany her articles showed her without a headscarf. She dreaded to think of the invective she would attract if she wrote under her real name. It was bad enough as it was, but if her haters knew that it was a half-Egyptian woman with a Jewish father (albeit an agnostic one), who was questioning and criticising their culture, history and institutions, it would no doubt be even worse. Her last piece, sarcastically titled: *Why everyone loves us (the English, of course),* had, at the more civilised end of the backlash, drawn the predictable suggestion that she might like to move somewhere else if she hated England so much.

She was sprung from her thoughts by Noah wandering into the kitchen and she gave him a hug, which he easily accepted.

'Hello, gorgeous. How was the football?'

'It got cancelled—we didn't have enough players.'

'Again? That's the second time this month, isn't it?'

'Yeah, too many flakes involved…'

'What do you fancy for tea? Puttanesca ok?'

'Mm, please. Have we got capers?'

'Of course, it's one crazy caper after another with us two pescatarians!' she said, squeezing him awkwardly to her side. He never felt awkward, however, about receiving her affection, whether it was in private or in public. He just enjoyed it. She was fully aware of how unusual this was for a boy of that age and never took it for granted. It wouldn't last forever.

'Have a look in the cupboard.'

He stooped down and peered inside for three seconds before saying,

'Can't see any…'

She stooped down beside him.

'What about these little tiddlers?' she said, plucking them out from behind a tin of carrot and butterbean soup.

'Are you hungry? Shall I put it on now?'

'Starving. Can I have some bread and hummus while I'm waiting?'

'Help yourself, but just one piece though'. She pointed towards the worktop. 'Look, someone found my purse and posted it back.'

He could tell she'd been crying and knew the reason why.

'Sweet. You love that purse. Uncle Ben gave it to you, didn't he?'

'He brought it back from Egypt when he went to see where Granddad's family had lived.'

He had heard about how his grandfather and his dad and all their Jewish friends were rounded up and thrown in jail and then forced to leave the country. He wondered if this was a good time to find out a bit more, but decided against it.

'Had anything been taken from your purse?'

'It don't think so. All the change was there and I can't remember if I had any notes in it. I wouldn't really care anyway. I'm just glad to have got it back.'

'Do you know who found it?'

'Somebody called Calum Roche.'

'It restores your faith in humanity, doesn't it, Mother?'

'Unfortunately, he didn't leave any contact details. It would have been nice to thank him.'

As Noah started to wander off towards his room she called after him.

'It's food tech tomorrow, isn't it? Have you got everything you need? I don't want to be having to pop out later on as you realize that you need some ground almonds and nutmeg at the last minute...'

'I'll check, but I think I'm ok—it's just fairy cakes, I think.'

After the puttanesca, and with Noah semi-engaging in his maths homework, she settled in at her desk to carry on with her latest piece. It was on the subject of English management. Looking over it again, she thought it still needed a bit of work. She wasn't happy with the title for a start:

Titanic failure: why are we so crap at management?

The content was pretty strong stuff, however, and would no doubt arouse the customary furious backlash from the usual quarters.

She still wrote the first draft by hand, which was more or less unheard of these days and, resuming work on it, she was struck by how childish and awkward her handwriting looked, especially in pencil—a bit like when you're shown an old postcard that you'd written to your grandparents as a child. She'd tried to hone a distinctive hand while at university, copying the Greek 'e' that her mother used in her lovely, arty, flowing hand, but she would intermittently lapse into the conventional 'e', revealing to the reader that the Greek 'e' was a contrivance.

Her eye skimmed over the text to the bits she wasn't sure about:

...Even our so-called finest hour, the Battle of Britain, wasn't exactly a rout— more of a plucky fending off, and roughly 20% of the pilots weren't British anyway. ...on the previous occasion our shores were under threat of imminent invasion, it was basically a storm that defeated the Spanish Armada rather than Sir Francis Drake, the fabled unflappable David Bryant of maritime mayhem.

It did seem like she was labouring the point somewhat, but on the other hand, she hadn't even properly touched on the inglorious way the Empire had been built up and then relinquished. She also wanted to include something about how the story of Scott's doomed Antarctic expedition seemed to encapsulate that particularly English combination of arrogance, complacency and the ability to spin foolish disaster into heroic failure. They had relied more on ponies than dogs and didn't really bother with furs or fixed hoods for God's sake!

When she had first thought of the idea for the piece, she had been banking on being able to carp about bungling preparations for the Olympics, but things surprisingly seemed to be going more or less to plan on that front. *On time and on budget* and all that. There was still plenty of time for things to go pear-shaped, however. She wondered whether she should hold her horses until then, but it was now too late to think of something else for this week and she'd already used her latest emergency piece last month. It wasn't like her not to have written a back-up straight away, but in a way, it was a good thing—a sign of progress in terms of bringing her diligence levels down to a healthier point. She could always work in a skit on the logo somewhere…

She was aware that she took this anti-Albion tack too often, but it had become her thing and had helped to make her name in the UK and had also landed her fairly regular articles overseas too.

Was she a broken record though? Was it all starting to come across as just a bit petty and peevish? Was she even wearing a bit thin to herself? Had she actually become Anglophobic? Was she also, therefore, contributing to the climate of hate and division herself? She felt like all of this might be true. She also felt as if she was betraying Noah a bit too. He supported the England sporting teams and generally had a positive view of the country. He wasn't really interested in what she wrote about, but she couldn't help feeling guilty that she was undermining something that was important to him and he was likely to become more aware of it as he got into his teens. She had also found herself feeling guilty for being peeved that there had been no major Olympic cock-ups to date. He was already quite excited about the whole thing—she had promised to try and get them tickets for one of the Team GB football games.

Part of what had driven her on was winding up the Boris Johnsons and White Van men of the world —and boy, did they need to be wound up and told a few home truths—even though it had potentially put her life in danger.

She'd always been a bit contrary; at Oxford, she'd once worn a Star of David T-shirt to a Labour club meeting when she thought things had been getting too relentlessly pro-Palestinian, and having always been staunchly pro-Republican, she found herself at times speaking up for the Unionist cause in her Irish Society discussions. It wasn't that she just liked playing devil's advocate; she felt that it was an instinctive reaction against easy and lazy group conformism towards certain views and stances. She deplored this herd mentality. Her mother said she got it from her Cork-born great nana, who would swear that black and tan was white rather than lose face once she'd stuck her neck out on something.

She thought back to the article that had first marked her out as one of the *bêtes noires* of Little England. It was a relatively tame piece provocatively entitled: ***Why isn't England a country?*** She didn't even see the line she'd taken as being particularly unpatriotic—the opposite, in fact, and she was actually proud of many aspects of British culture. She was ethnically half-British after all, and she definitely felt more British than Egyptian. A few weeks previously, 'in the interest of balance', she'd written an 'article' entitled: ***Greater Britain,*** which merely consisted of a list of all the British people and organisations she could think of that merited the title of 'great.'

The list, of course, drew as much criticism for its omissions—many of them conscious—as it did for its inclusiveness, but she'd nailed her colours to the mast, generated plenty of debate and brought some unfairly overlooked female figures to public attention.

Her underlying agenda was that the British and, in particular, the English needed to face up to the reality of their history and national character. A reckless, arrogant and puerile mentality seemed to have become the template that too many people struggled to grow out of. It underpinned the dominant discourse in society and she foresaw the country spiraling in on itself and disintegrating.

She limited herself to one piece a month along these lines in her main serious column and focused on the topical political stuff the rest of the time. It was a kind of crusade for her and she felt very fortunate to have been given the platform. Nobody else was doing anything remotely like it in the mainstream press.

Fortunately, the editor, Sally, despised the *Daily Mail* and the other right-wing papers too. She was determined to counteract their agenda wherever possible and help to redress what she saw as a huge imbalance between the influence of right- and left-wing commentators in the British media.

One of Anna's former colleagues on another paper had told her that there was a rumour going round that the only reason that she got away with being so self-indulgent in her columns was that Sally fancied her. It did make her think, but she knew she'd earned her corn and paid her dues on the regionals and periodicals and got the position on merit. What's more, she was only more or less following the brief that she'd set out in her interview. She wouldn't be surprised if Sally did fancy her. They'd met up that afternoon to touch base and the slightly too early home-made birthday card she had given her was way over the top—it was as if she'd spent a whole evening on it—with drawings, photos and a collage.

However, as a female journalist, Anna also had the USP of being equally at ease writing about politics, sport or culture. Sally was getting three journalists for the price of one. She was as comfortable writing a *Wags to witches* story as she was putting the bitch into an ex-Tory minister's obituary. In her occasional private moments of self-eulogising bombast, she liked to think that she bestrode the paper like a golden-thighed colossus who could be on every series of *Question Time* if she chose to.

When Sally hired her, she knew the agenda that Anna was going to pursue flew in the face of the dominant media discourse of blowing Britain's own trumpet and putting Johnny Foreigner down, and that it would really ruffle some major feathers. She wasn't wrong. Even some of their own readers didn't like it. The fairly innocuous line of debunking national myths like British understatement, the Bulldog spirit and stiff-upper-lip didn't go down well in certain quarters, but once you started challenging Blighty's glorious past, you opened yourself up to a whole new world of verbal slings and arrows. Sally, to her credit, however, had never asked her to tone it down or change tack. Yet.

With anything factual, you had to be absolutely spot on with your facts and she had gained a first in history at Oxford. Had she not become disenchanted with the dry dustiness of academia, she could quite easily have gone on to do a doctorate and probably become an expert in any era she'd chosen to. She was therefore on pretty solid ground in that respect, but still double- or triple-checked anything remotely contentious.

She would have preferred not to have a photo accompanying her column due to the threats she received, but it had been there from day one, so there was little point in removing it at this stage.

Although her parents weren't aware of the full extent of the bile that was directed at their daughter, they knew enough to be concerned about it and wished she would steer clear of the deliberately provocative stuff. Her history of recalcitrance, however, meant that they knew that there was no point in them going on at her about it as it would only serve to spur her on, so they generally bit their tongues. For her part, Anna had also managed to refrain from pointing out that she was probably just as likely to be randomly blown up on a Tube train or a bus these days. They'd been through more than enough with Ben, so she had also never mentioned that the police had given her a mirror on a stick to check for bombs under her car or that all her post was scanned for suspect content.

She had Noah to think about too, of course, especially now that he was becoming more independent. She worried about him whenever they were apart and was never happier than when she had him safely ensconced at home with her.

Maybe it was time to quit while she was ahead and scale back the 'history lessons'? She could just do that sort of stuff occasionally perhaps—maybe once or twice a year? Would that make any difference? She did feel as if she had got most of her longstanding bugbears off her chest anyway. There was something addictive about it though—the adrenaline surge that provocation afforded her. She also didn't want to be seen to be letting the bullyboys get their way, but maybe it was time to call it a day—she'd done her bit, stuck her head over the parapet. Only the other week, a female Labour MP had been attacked with a knife in her surgery.

Fortunately, due to the concerns she'd had from the beginning, she'd managed to persuade Sally to use an oldish photo that didn't really look like her that much. It also made her look more attractive than she actually was. Her hair was down and, of course, a face-on photo gave no indication of the full extent of her nose. Aquiline was the kindest way she'd heard it described—at least it made it sound distinctive.

As the flames rose to her Roman nose and her hearing aid started to melt.

She had some idea how Joan of Arc felt.

She'd overheard Gavin at the party where she'd met him saying that he was keen on the Mediterranean type. A lot of people had assumed that she was of Italian or French origin before she'd started wearing headscarves.

The pang she'd felt at the thought that she'd lost his number had revealed to her that she was pretty keen on him, but there was still a nagging suspicion that he was probably too good to be true anyway.

He hadn't called her though, and she'd seen him put the number in his phone. Five days had gone by. Maybe he didn't want to seem too keen, but two or three days would have done the trick. He didn't seem that type, though; he came across as sensitive but straightforward. No subterfuge or subtext—ostensibly at least. She'd been so taken with him that when she'd made her customary, but now sober, version of the Irish exit, she'd allowed herself the seedy extravagance of a late-night cab home, something that she normally found would dampen a night out, but, which, in this case, she felt could be overridden by her exceptionally good mood.

She had no qualms about making the running in relationships herself, but something was holding her back. Could it have something to do with his name?

Hi. This is my partner, Gavin.

She couldn't actually ever imagine herself saying that, but was she that shallow?

Her ex-husband had been an Ian, but she'd overlooked that as he bore a more than passing resemblance to Michael Praed in *Robin of Sherwood*. His name was Ian Finlay and she had been besotted with him, despite the lukewarm reception that he had been accorded by most of her family and friends. They'd met not long after uni, when she was dealing with the onset of her drink problems and his laid-back, new-age approach to life was a great counterpoint to her ridiculous work ethic and ultra-conscientiousness.

Time revealed, however, that rather than being a freewheeling breath of fresh air, he was more of a bullshitting idler; a struggling artist whom she would basically have to support and mother for the best part of four years, even though she had plenty of her own issues to deal with. A man who, at weekends, or when they were on holiday together, refused to leave the house in the morning until he had evacuated his bowels; a process which sometimes necessitated a wait of several hours and which had put the kibosh on any more holidays with friends or family after a disastrous trip to Brittany with her brother and his partner.

His thing artistically was animals out of context and, at first, she'd been amused by the humour and impressed by his technical skills, but it wasn't long before she realised that he only managed to produce about four or five pieces a year. If he was lucky, he'd sell two or three of those but then would have to give fifty per cent to the small gallery in Whitechapel that sold them and as they only sold for around six hundred pounds a time, it didn't amount to much of a contribution to their income.

Another problem was that he was falling between two stools and putting himself in too niche a market. People who liked animal art wanted more conventional settings and those who weren't keen on animal art obviously weren't interested, but he wouldn't change tack. He wouldn't compromise and do stuff that he wasn't interested in just to make money. She'd respected his artistic integrity in the first year or two, but then gradually became irritated by his stubbornness and satisfaction with the way things were going, especially when she realized that he spent most of the day fiddling around on one of his guitars or watching *The Sopranos*. He would also have let her do the lion's share of the housework if she'd allowed him to. It wasn't as if he was breaking radical new ground artistically either—it was often just stuff like a bull in a china shop or a fish out of water. Beautifully painted and occasionally with a novel twist, but not exactly the shock of the new. There was certainly no high artistic principle at stake—he was going nowhere and it gradually became apparent that he was never going to change. Although her dad had never had much time for him, Ian had succeeded in charming her mother somewhat, but even the benefit of her doubt ran out in the end.

They'd had the whole big white wedding and everything too, which she had never really been bothered about and mainly did in order to please her mother, who surprisingly ended up not taking over all the preparations, although at times Anna wished she had.

How could she have got it so wrong? How could she have seriously thought he was her soul mate? Had she just viewed him through rosé-coloured spectacles? At least he'd given her Noah, who had inherited his dad's good looks, but none of his idling flakiness—at least not yet. Maybe that would burst out when he hit his teens? Ian had shown increasingly less interest in Noah and now spent more or less half of his time in Kyoto with his Japanese yoga-teacher girlfriend. In the end, the final word on her ex had gone to her younger brother Dan, who had quipped that she would need to go to *Ian Finlay and beyond* to find 'the one' This had since become a bit of a family joke when Noah wasn't around—although he'd actually overheard it one evening when his Uncle Dan had got a bit loud at a dinner party while he was off playing Fifa in his room. He didn't mind, in fact he thought it was pretty funny. He didn't take his dad too seriously himself and he loved his Uncle Dan and would forgive him almost anything.

Noah seemed to have very low expectations of his dad, so anything bordering on adequate was a bonus. He generally treated Ian the way a wise, loving and infinitely patient grandparent might tolerate and indulge a wayward toddler. He called him Ian rather than Dad and although his dad didn't seem to mind, as he'd also been on first name terms with his own mother and father, he would sometimes call Noah 'son' as that was what his dad had often used with him.

These days, Anna very much doubted that there was such a thing as *the one* for most people—more like a series of *ones* that eventually fizzled out or blew up in your face. She didn't want a succession of men traipsing through Noah's life or traipsing through her life for that matter. Some people seemed to find it, but was it just a case of their relationships surviving by dint of sacrifice and self-denial? Or just being too lazy or scared to aim for something better?

She'd instantly felt very comfortable around Gavin—he had an ease, maturity and wit. Maybe she could call him G. *For God's sake, woman, get a grip! You've only met him twice.* She went to the kitchen to make a cup of tea.

She'd only been in three proper long-term relationships, but having grown up with two brothers and also worked in several male-dominated environments, she always half-expected a crucial flaw or weakness to reveal itself at some point. Strangely, part of the problem was that, for all his faults, she'd never met a man that she got on better with or who had made her laugh more than Ben. Any suitor would have to measure up to him and his premature demise meant that his reputation was set in stone, never to be undone.

It was, of course, far too early to tell if G was just very good at putting on a front and sometimes you just don't realise until it's too late…

As she was absently stirring the bag around in the cup, she heard the plaintive, baby seagull call that the internal plumbing of the fridge sometimes made and looked across at the digital clock on the oven. The time changed from 6.29 to 6.30 at that precise moment. Life counting down. At night, when she glanced at her radio alarm clock as she was getting ready for bed, it would often say 11.11. It felt like it had some sort of fateful significance to it, but she suspected that it signified nothing more than the fact that she normally went to bed around that time.

Before she knew it, Noah would be going off to uni—everybody said that the secondary school years just fly by. She needed to savour this time. She absolutely loved the relationship she had with him—he was her best friend in the world. She was more successful than she'd ever dreamed of work-wise, but if she was honest with herself, she wasn't fulfilled. The third pillar of her life was missing. Success didn't necessarily bring happiness. Happiness itself was success. She'd kind of known this since reading *Winnie the Pooh* as a child. Pooh Bear didn't have a drink problem, though. Had she become Rabbit? Rabbit crossed with Owl?

She should call him now. Strike while the iron's hot.

But even as she was saying it to herself, she knew that she wouldn't just go and do it straight away, as she would have done in the past. It felt like something had shifted, was shifting, inside her. Or was it just that she couldn't be bothered with it all? Or that she knew it would complicate things and mean less time with Noah?

She gazed out at the backs of the houses opposite and could see a topless woman through the frosted glass of a bathroom window. Surely she knew that people could see in?

She was conscious that she hadn't been aroused by this image, which, though slightly pixelated, was still objectively attractive and since the easily dismissible teen fumblings with a close friend at school, she'd sometimes wondered if she had, in fact, any leanings of that nature. She was all too aware that you couldn't control what feelings or longings may emerge—sexuality, like most things, was beyond your control.

She just needed to phone him.

Should she follow her gut? What was her gut actually saying? Was her gut even reliable? Was she still being too head-led as usual?

The topless woman had gone. As she sipped her tea and stared at the swaying poplar trees shaking off their leaves above the tops of the houses, some lines she'd read at sixth form surfaced in her mind:

On the surge-ride of elation, weightless,
Body simply the armature of energy
In that earliest sea-freedom, the savage amazement of life,
The salt mouthful of actual existence,
With strength like light—

She still had strength like light at times. She hadn't had a drink in over twelve years.

She had been the destroyer of shadows, the one who *could* always be bothered, the one with the acute sense of time, who could remember everything. The drinking had provided some welcome relief from all that unbearable clarity and lightness and then when that had got out of control, she'd lost herself in her work and Noah and held it together, starting from scratch every day, the thirst always there, dancing in her veins, but less than it would be after the next drink.

She had somehow become both indomitable and self-destructive. How had that happened? She'd built herself a carapace—she'd had to, but was in danger of becoming hardened all the way through in some ways.

She needed to lose herself in love again now, to see *the eye of ravenous joy*, to let herself go. *In the flashing expanse, the bloom of sea-life.*

It was time.

She'd finish her tea, do some yoga, have a long bath and give him a call.

Speak to Sally too. No rush though.

Take your time.

Sink into the moment.

Breathe.

Ruthless and marmoreal no more, Anna
Ruthless and marmoreal no more.

16

Thursday

As David King sat slumped on the verandah overlooking his plantation, a disconcerting gurgling noise emanated from his bowels. As the sound and accompanying bloated sensation increased in intensity, he staggered inside to the bathroom to relieve the pressure on his bladder.

Looking in the mirror, he saw two horizontal slits barred by rows of vertical, black stitches where his eyes should have been. On closer examination, he realized that the dark eyelashes on his upper eyelids had been knotted to those of his lower lids.

He was feeling acute discomfort in his groin and, looking down, was strangely unalarmed to see nothing other than a luxuriant pubic mound. Then, just as he was wondering how he was actually able to see anything with his eyes stitched closed, the pressure and pain became immense and a moist, pale pink water balloon emerged from between his legs. Dropping down in slow motion, the skin membrane reverberated on soft impact with the grass that had appeared beneath his feet —cushioning the foetus huddled peacefully within.

When Dave awoke, he was not surprised to discover that he was lying on his back. His grandma had warned him when he was a boy that sleeping that way gave you nightmares, and personal experience had borne this out.

He sat up, swung his legs round onto the bedroom floor and, swivelling on the edge of the bed as he did so, was pleased to observe that he had left no skid mark on the cover sheet in the process.

Still reeling from the dream, he padded into the bathroom, flipped his clammy genitals over the lip of the sink, set the cold tap running and splashed his tired trinity several times to revive himself. He'd heard that it boosted virility—apparently, the Romans had had fertility problems due to their fondness of hot baths. He also avoided anything minty for the same reason.

He examined himself in his full-length mirror. Humans were freaky-looking things. Like aliens. Why the big mop of hair on the head with tufts here and there? Imagine an animal like that. Women were especially freaky—a shock of long hair at the top of an otherwise mostly hairless body. An ape like that would be considered revolting—like it had been shaved all over except for the top of its head.

He then did his usual twenty chin-ups, holding on to the bathroom door frame with his fingertips. He made sure his chin reached frame level each time. even though he'd had another bad night's sleep.

He'd been plagued by insomnia since before his teens. It could probably be traced back to a sordid row between his parents that had woken him up in the middle of the night. Something that he couldn't quite grasp had gone on between his mother and a man called Barry and there was some kind of film she'd appeared in and his father was now threatening to throw her out of the house naked. They seemed to be down at the bottom of the stairs by the front door and his mum was sobbing desperately until finally his dad relented and told her that it didn't matter and that he'd had dozens of women himself.

He'd just lain there frozen, listening to the whole thing unfold without intervening and had never told his younger sisters and brother about it. It had since crossed his mind that he might have dreamed it all, but it was vivid and disturbing in a way that was surely beyond the imagination of a kid that age. His parents had often argued quite loudly during the day while he was around—mainly about money and often on a Saturday morning after his mum had revealed that the housekeeping money issued on Thursday had already been spent—but this was on a whole different level. It was probably the defining moment of his life and he'd not even told the only real confidante he'd had in life—his ex, Beth—any of the details.

It was not long after this that he'd tried to copy one of the older lads who lived on the same estate and carve a swastika with a razor blade into his forearm. He'd only got as far as one horizontal bar when blood started to pour out and he'd had to quickly sneak downstairs and out of the front door of the house before coming back round and in through the back, pretending that he'd cut it on some glass. He was worried that they'd be dubious that he could have accidentally cut it in that part of his forearm, but fortunately he encountered his mum first, who was loading the washing machine at the time and, falling for it without question, put a bandage on it. He still bore the scar, though it had now shrunk and faded.

Insomnia had probably played some part in the secret breakdown that he'd had at the age of sixteen. It had come about in strange circumstances… Still awake a couple of hours after having taken out the earpiece and turned off his radio at the end of John Peel, he'd got up to go to the toilet. Normally, when standing at the pan, he wouldn't place the soles of his feet flat on the cold, tiled bathroom floor. He'd curl his toes down and balance on the outside edges of his feet. On this particular occasion, however, he decided to 'be a man' and fully put his feet flat down on the cold floor. Weirdly, after about ten seconds his legs started to shake inexplicably and reverting to his customary foot position didn't make it stop. He finished peeing and went back to bed, but the shaking continued and when deep breathing didn't make it go away, a feeling of panic set in. He tried walking up and down in his room to make it wear off and then sought reassurance by asking himself what the worst that could happen was—he'd have a terrible night's sleep and he was used to that, he could deal with it and the shaking was bound to stop at some point.

*Don't worry, you're a rock, you're the rock of the family,
you can beat it.*

As he'd often done during sleepless nights when assailed
by dark thoughts, he remembered the defiance of Steve
McQueen in *Papillon* shouting, '*Hey, you bastards, I'm still
here*' and Robert De Niro in *Raging Bull* repeating, '*You
never got me down, Ray. You never got me down.*'

Something then occurred to his contrary mind and a
demon voice piped up: *Don't think you're safe, matey boy.
You might kill yourself. What if you go mad and kill
yourself? You can't control that. What if you go mad and
kill yourself?*

Kill yourself. Kill yourself. Kill yourself.

Kill yourself.

He didn't have the urge to kill himself, but the voice
couldn't be silenced. It was like trying not to think of a pink
elephant. The trouble with paranoia was that when you've
mentally eliminated all the external threats, you turn on
yourself and there's no lasting refuge from this internal
assailant. You can go for months without remembering, but
then out of nowhere, you remember that you've forgotten.
It's always only a single thought away – waiting to jump out
at you. On the way home the other day, he'd been on the
platform watching the 5.40 roll slowly in when it crossed
his mind whether the driver was always worried that
someone was going to throw themselves in front of the train
as they approached. And then he thought that he could do it
now, just lose control for a second and do it and then it
would be done. He had to move to the back of the platform
and hold on to a lamppost and half turn his back to the track
to make sure he didn't.

Somehow, he'd got through the night of the breakdown
and fallen asleep for a few hours. The feeling of panic was
still there in the morning, however, and though the physical
shaking had stopped, there was a constant, strong
background buzz of the hollow, watery feeling in his legs
that you get when you have a brush with death or a big
fright. White noise in his veins.

He didn't tell anyone about it. It was as if he was a bomb-proof underground bunker which had absorbed an explosion from within its own walls, leaving no sign from the outside of what had taken place inside.

He battled with the empty panic and demon voice in private for the best part of ten years until he met Beth, and then it more or less went away in a matter of months.

The insomnia remained an issue, however, and, rather like when you realise that you've managed to block out a noise that was keeping you awake and therefore become aware of it again, the demon voice would, occasionally, from nowhere, in the dead of night, as she lay beside him, whisper potentially fatal words. At least in recent years, he had learned to nap during the day, balm his hurt mind and *knit up the raveled sleeve of care*.

Now a divorced father of one, he had recently discovered that listening to podcasts would often send him off to sleep after a while. It was a win-win situation, as he either fell asleep quite quickly or learned some interesting information about more or less any topic he was interested in—history, politics, philosophy, sport, literature and science—and as a rule, he eventually drifted off anyway after a few hours. It was the boredom as much as anything that had been the killer and the podcasts at least took this out of the equation. Plus, he was learning something into the bargain. Once in a while, though, nothing would work—he'd be tired but not at all sleepy. Thankfully, however, he could generally rely on the fact that, by a certain point in the week, the cumulative exhaustion would have become so great that a decent night's sleep would eventually come.

Dave's great hope was that he would come to be perceived as something of a tormented Renaissance man that nobody could pigeon-hole. How many people who'd read all the works of Evelyn Waugh could also do fifty one-arm press ups? He liked to joke that his dad had been a man for all seasons—the rugby season, the football season and the cricket season, but he saw himself as being a bit more multi-faceted than his old man.

Since his wife had left him, he had been channelling his post-break-up energies into a number of projects, namely, completing his self-help book/manifesto, *The English Manual*, rising to the rank of Captain in the TA and tracking down Anna Heron.

Things had got a bit ragged around the edges in his life in recent years, but the book was the thread that was keeping him going. All told, it had been around five years in the making and the second draft was now more or less finished.

It dealt clearly and concisely with three main subjects:

1. The erosion of English culture.
2. Resisting the emasculation of the modern male.
3. The rebirth of Albion.

He had wanted it to be a right-wing version of one of Orwell's books of essays, in that it dealt with an unlikely range of subjects; from the fairly mundane *How to avoid getting ill*—which he believed his exemplary sickness record made him an expert on—to the profoundly philosophical and political *The Nature of Nature*. Curiously, he was most pleased with the middle part, which hadn't even been part of his original plan—it had just turned out that a lot of his notes pertained to that subject. The section was designed to guide his fellow countrymen through the ins and outs of dealing with the opposite sex.

He'd thought about presenting it in A to Z form, but realized that he would never have enough topics to cover the whole alphabet and in the end he'd opted for a series of simple themes with headings such as: 'Attraction', 'Control' and 'Deception', under which he'd arranged observations and pointers such as:

Be aware that often when an unknown female returns your look, it is not necessarily because she is interested in you; it is likely to be because she is checking, out of pure vanity, whether you are still admiring her.

To a large extent, female arousal has little to do with the attractiveness of her partner, as it is largely governed by the state of her hormones at any given time.

The root of most women's frustration in relationships stems from the fact that the men they are most attracted to make the most unsuitable partners.

Women seek a master only to turn him into a slave.

You will need to choose between an interesting woman and a tidy house.

Though your wife and children will have equal standing in your life, you will always play second fiddle to the children in her eyes.

If women were physically stronger than men, they would be kicking seven shades out of their partners most days of the week.

He'd inserted one of his own poems at the beginning of each chapter of the book: *I am Winter*, *Rebel without applause* and *The wind will be our anthem*, and although intended primarily for a male audience, he felt that women could also benefit from the self-enlightenment that his insights would provide.

One such woman was the journalist Anna Heron. She embodied everything he despised about modern society— pro-migrant, pro-EU, feminist, metropolitan and leftist. He'd briefly been a communist in his youth and flirted with various far-left organisations, but had then gradually come to the opinion that the right was right because they had nature on their side. He'd always been sceptical about democracy because he felt that it was at the mercy of the establishment and big business, but now it was also because he believed that most people were politically ignorant or too easily influenced and couldn't be relied on to make the best choices.

His views had further hardened since Beth had cheated on him. He'd always suspected that she had never really loved him, that she had just initially been kind of intrigued by him and gone along with his advances until she had somehow gradually slid into a steady relationship with him. Then, further down the line, he just happened to be her partner at the time she felt that she ought to be settling down and then decided that it might as well be him as another. There was never anything to indicate that he was her type, but he loved her in his own way and was prepared to overlook the doubts that he had about her feelings for him— or at least push them to the back of his mind. He managed to suppress them most of the time, but if she took against him in any kind of dispute (which she often did), the anger would explode in a way that Beth would find frightening and disturbing, but which was actually only about a three on Dave's rage-o-meter.

They'd travelled a lot and got on really well before Jake was born, but things started to deteriorate about a year later and the bickering became almost constant.

Since she'd left him, he'd lost touch with most of the mutual friends that they'd had while they were married, which had come as no surprise to him. He'd avoided putting all his eggs in her basket friend-wise, and had continued to go out fairly regularly with his TA mates. If he was honest, though, he had reservations about almost all of them to some extent—he found it difficult to overlook flaws in people's characters. They were either a bit tight, too full of themselves or at a different point of the political spectrum. He'd made more of an effort with them since the break-up, but couldn't help feeling a bit transparent about it. He still enjoyed the banter, though, but there was one guy, who was the epitome of the long-winded bluntness that flourished in this part of the world and if he knew he was going to be there, he'd make sure that he arrived slightly late and sit away from him.

He felt as if he was living a double life. The only human softness left now was for his son, but now Jake was growing up, he could already feel them growing apart. He'd had to accept that his son was basically a mummy's boy. Beth had always made sure that he was closer to her. He had been slow to realise that there had been a competition going on from the word go and that he was coming a poor second. Then she cheated on him, got custody of Jake and took the dog too. Before the settlement, there'd been periods when she wouldn't give him access and he'd nearly gone out of his mind, but then, when he actually got to see Jake, it was never as good as he'd hoped it would be. He no longer minded not seeing him one weekend out of four; it just felt like hard work a lot of the time. Dave liked to think he was in touch with his feminine side a bit, but he was realising that he was too hard-edged for Jake, who wasn't really into the macho things that he was into, like boxing and rugby.

The concept of hardness was something that had long preoccupied Dave, the key question being whether it was harder to feel pain and not show it or to hardly feel the pain at all. He also had a theory that the people who were apparently the hardest emotionally were actually the softest underneath and had had to develop a thick shell to protect themselves.

'Hardness' was very much a working-class preoccupation and classwise, he felt as if he had fallen between two stools. Although he could relate to both in certain ways, he wasn't either properly working class or middle class, but he had come to accept that he was probably more lower-middle class than upper working class. Basically, however, middle-class people saw him as a bit working class and working-class people saw him as middle class. He'd definitely become more middle class since he went to uni and generally felt a bit guilty about it—about listening to Radio 4, reading broadsheets and losing most of his accent.

Once when he was down in London while Beth was doing her internship, he'd head-butted a guy from Guildford at a party who'd called him *a posh Northern wanker.* He was on a hair trigger for anything like that, but the weird thing was that he now probably felt more at ease around middle-class people, and if he was honest with himself, he preferred the broadsheets to the tabloids these days (he'd grown up with the *Daily Express*). It was through this broadening out of his reading that Anna Heron had come to his attention, as she was countering more or less everything that he believed in. She was the epitome of the Brit-bashing, multiculturalist, eco-friendly, lefty liberal, who went out of her way to put the country down at every opportunity.

He loved his country with a deep, visceral passion that just had to be natural and right. Surely the pure, raw emotion of singing the national anthem had to be drawn from a deep well of natural human feeling? How could that spine-tingling, tears-streaming-down-your-face feeling of belonging to something so great and special be wrong?

As he now saw it, however, the time had come for England to go its own way, to go it alone and jettison the Scots, Welsh and Northern Irish, get out of the EU, get back to basics and build things up from scratch again.

I think our country sinks beneath the yoke.
It weeps, it bleeds and each new day a gash
Is added to her wounds.

He was realistic enough to realise that it couldn't be the same olde England, of course—the huge influx of Irish and other blood over one hundred and fifty years had seen to that. He once saw an old interview with Michael Caine where he was saying that the Celt was self-destructive, unlike the Anglo-Saxon. He'd probably been talking about people like Richard Burton, Richard Harris and Peter O'Toole, but he was right; Britain had gone from being the workshop of the world to a nation of mouthy, prancing, posing entertainers. John Lennon, Johnny Rotten, Boy George, Morrissey, the Gallagher brothers. Troubadours and jesters. All mouth and no trousers. Or all mouth and trousers, as it used to be…The country had been too de-anglicised to make an industrious, scrupulous and thrifty England possible again, but a new brand of Englishness could emerge, brimming with creativity, enterprise and freedom, rising up and spreading its wings to take its place at the world's top table once again.

For people like Anna Heron, though, England wasn't even a country. How could it not be a country? It had a flag, a Queen, a football and rugby team. Not only was it a country, it was a country that had created the greatest empire the world had ever seen. It had also more or less created the modern world: steam engines, trains, electricity, the jet engine and the Internet and then given it its common language. The Scots had played their part, of course, he could see that, but it was the English who had created the environment for them to thrive in. Then, weeping with no more worlds to conquer, they had handed over the sceptre of world domination to the American younger brother that had outgrown it.

Dave couldn't understand why Heron hated England so much. His Glaswegian uncle Gordon was the same—always sniping and wanting them to fail at sport. He would support Scotland against other teams if the Scots supported England, but there was no chance of that happening, so why should he bother?

Although he approved of it, due to the fear it must induce in her, he did not, however, indulge in the online abuse and death threats Heron received. He was playing the long game. He was the lone wolf that leaves no tracks. The eagle soaring high above its prey—unseen.

He had never been affiliated to any of the political organisations that shared his views and since a colleague had, fortunately, mentioned that the security services were all over that sort of online stuff like a rash, he had continued to avoid accessing any of their sites. No Facebook or Twitter either. He'd even gone to the trouble of hiding the memory stick containing *The English Manual* under the hook panel in one of the shoeboxes where he kept some of his old fishing tackle in his garage, the threshold of which boasted a union flag doormat which he would wipe his feet on before entering. (He would actually have liked to have had a pop-out doormat to wipe his feet on before getting into his Rover and it had even crossed his mind to approach a car manufacturer with the concept, although he suspected that they would just ignore him and then go ahead and rip off the idea).

He had a thing about shoeboxes—he never really liked to throw them away when they were good quality, so he had several under his bed with bits and bobs in as well as a few in the garage. He liked tins too. He didn't really collect them as such, but had accumulated a fair few. Closing a tin or a shoebox gave him great satisfaction—much more than opening one did. Closing any lid was a pleasure, but this hadn't stopped him getting annoyed when Beth left the lids off the toothpaste or marmite. If he brought it up, she'd just say, 'Well, you enjoy closing stuff, don't you? I'm doing you a favour.' She always had an answer.

The police wouldn't find anything directly incriminating re Anna Heron in any of his tins or boxes and there was no wall covered in her photos or articles of hers covered in scrawled obscenities.

The problem for him was that she had a similar MO. She left no trail. He assumed from the one picture of her in the public domain that she was Jewish and gathered from his online research that Anna Heron couldn't be her real name.

He'd spoken to his brother-in-law, a London-based pap, about where the hacks hung out now that Fleet Street was no more, and had casually dropped her name into the conversation. She didn't seem to be a regular at the haunts where her colleagues drank and was apparently hardly ever seen in the office. Columnists normally worked from home these days anyway.

She did live somewhere, though, and went out every day to the shops, to a cafe or for a stroll in the park. He'd read all her articles looking for clues. He'd be able to read her latest offering on the train down to London. She was out there somewhere. Thinking she was safe, that she was the smart one.

He'd fantasised about getting a terminal illness and going round systematically blowing up the offices of the *Guardian*, the BBC, the Labour Party and the *Daily Mirror*—striking a blow against the liberal-left Goliath—but, for the time being, he'd focus on her. He wasn't even sure yet exactly what he was going to do. He would cross that bridge when he came to it—sometimes the plan needed to be loose and flexible, with room for improvisation. The ideal scenario would be to engineer an encounter with her in a high place and then let gravity—with a helping hand from him—take its course. He just had an overwhelming urge to do something: to track her down, to scare her, at the very least. He just needed to be wary of CCTV as he went about his business.

Where there was a will, there was a way.

8

Since he'd split up with Rachel two and a half years previously, Calum Roche hadn't been in any relationships. He hadn't even been on a date or had a drunken snog.

He'd always been adamant that he would never get divorced, as he'd been on the receiving end of what it can do to kids—especially if it isn't handled in a mature and amicable fashion. The thing was, although it takes two to tango, it only takes one to untangle.

He'd thought that the love, care, patience, compromise and emotional intelligence involved in successful parental monogamy made it the pinnacle of civilisation, so now one of the main raisons d'être of his life was in tatters.

After Rachel and he had split up, he'd harboured hopes of them getting back together once she'd realized that other men were even worse than he was. However, unfortunately for him, her new man, Richard, seemed, so far at least, to be one of the good ones—seemingly honest, supportive, sensitive and, decisively, not steeped in the negativity, defensive pessimism and contrariness that had been Calum's undoing. She was contrary too, however, and any marriage where contrariness has become the main trait that you have in common is obviously doomed to failure.

He'd tried to change. He saw himself as being on something of a perpetual self-improvement programme, but the occasional major lapse was always going to be inevitable.

He had hoped that the fact that he felt that he was harder on himself than on others excused him to a certain extent, but ironically, the feeling of never being good enough or doing things well enough had eventually proved to be true for his marriage. It was also ironic that what led to his downfall in the relationship was his irritation with the fact that, in his eyes, she was also very negative and critical, but refused to acknowledge it. It galled him how lacking in self-awareness and forgiving of herself she could be, so he decided to keep a secret record of all the negative comments and criticisms of him that she made in order to present her with it the next time they had that argument. He did question whether this was a good idea, but in the end never actually got the chance to play his trump card anyway as she found the list one afternoon tucked inside a copy of *The Outsider* when she was sorting out books to take to the charity shop. And that was that.

By now he'd realized, and had come to terms with the fact, that they weren't getting back together. He'd often said that the two great lessons of life were that change is the only constant and everything is relative, and now, inevitably, he was the victim of one of his own dictums.

In the initial aftermath of the split, in an effort to help himself to get over her, he'd consciously tried to remind himself of all the little things around the house that had irritated him about her, but it had failed to ease the pain. Even the recollection of her compulsive placing of square or rectangular objects at an angle of forty-five degrees on a shelf or other surface no longer bothered him—the petty twelve-year cold war of adjusting and readjusting inanimate objects was now over. He had come in a distant second in a two-horse race. He'd have to steer any future partner in the direction of circular objects to avoid a repeat of this scenario.

Before things turned sour, they'd sometimes joked that marriage was a struggle to the death, but for them, it had turned out to be a struggle until early middle age. Their instincts had always been in opposition to each other and over the years he'd often found himself humming, *You and I travel to the beat of a different drum* around the house and wondered if Rachel had ever picked up on it. Opposites attract, apparently, but in the long term, if both parties are stubborn and refuse to let the other get the upper hand, it's going to founder. He had also long been aware that her love for him was tenuous and that there had never been any deep, animal attraction to him. It was conditional on his behaviour and on his level of devotion to her. She generally liked him—in an objective way and she had felt genuine love for him at times, but ultimately it was still conditional and any sign that she wasn't *the one* for him could turn it to indifference and even hatred, and naturally, his awareness of this made it more difficult for him to adore her.

When the other big dreams of his youth hadn't materialised, he'd clung to the belief that he could still at least make a success of marriage and parenthood. The trouble was, the only real lessons you receive in the marital arts are from your parents and if they weren't that proficient at it, you were in trouble.

Now he was just trying to make up for being a dick to his daughters' mum by making a success of the divorce and being a decent father to them through these difficult years.

The upside of the situation was that he felt like he had more time to devote to them, and more time on his hands in general—the luxury of boredom. The downside was, of course, that he saw less of them. The other downside was that he was basically lonely. He needed a companion—someone to take him out of himself.

Time to put himself out there again. But it was so difficult to meet people even in a city of eight million souls. Could he really be bothered?

There were no options at work, as the staff was too small and the turnover too slow, but a couple of female colleagues had urged him to try a particular dating site that had worked out well for friends of theirs. What did he have to lose—apart from a bit of money and pride? The whole thing was far riskier for women and there was a much greater chance that they'd be lumbered with an idiot for the evening. It was amazing that any of them even bothered. You had to admire their optimism. *Vive the triumph of hope over experience...*

He'd done a bit of research and it seemed that there were more men signed up to these sites than women and as the women who had signed up were much choosier about who'd they'd agree to meet, the odds weren't in his favour. The colleagues reassured him, however, that, in their experience, most men were terrible at dating and fell into the obvious traps of not asking any questions, not listening properly and talking about themselves too much, so there was no reason why he shouldn't do alright if he bore this in mind.

All he needed to do, therefore—as long as he was meeting someone vaguely compatible—was relax, ask questions, listen to the answers and be good-humoured. He knew it was time to dip his wing in the water, but everything about it felt against the grain. He thought he might be alright once he'd actually got someone to go on the date with him, but he couldn't imagine coming up with a profile or picture that would appeal to someone that he would be interested in.

He grabbed a can of Guinness from the fridge, logged into his laptop, and as he waited for it to open up, satisfyingly teased a crow from his left nostril with the nail of his index finger and examined it. It was embedded with a few nasal hairs, giving it the appearance of a mini, dried, green anchovy. He rolled it a little between his middle finger and thumb and then flicked it towards the wastepaper basket by the door, betting himself that if he managed to get it in, it would mean that the whole dating thing would work out. It landed right on the rim and stuck there. Did that count? He told himself that it did, though he suspected that it didn't.

An hour later, having successfully signed up and posted his profile, and realising all he had in the fridge was some well out-of-date peppered salmon, he popped out to get something to eat.

Passing his car a little way down the street, he noticed that someone had written something in the dust on the lower part of the passenger side doors.

He stooped down to look at it.

In a neat hand it said:

Doce Nos Viam Bonam
The motto of his primary school, St Boniface's.
Teach us the right way.

He gave what he hoped was a wry smile and walked on.

11

Friday October 1st

Calum's fears that something more sinister was going on weren't allayed by the fact that he'd finally had a text back from Ally, which strongly suggested that he wasn't the one behind all the messages. He did actually seem to be in Australia and had found the whole thing funny.

Fortunately, the imminent prospect of a date was serving as a welcome distraction. October already. Things had started happening a lot quicker than he'd imagined— some people didn't muck about. He had a date already—for that evening!

Was he nervous about it? Was he worrying about it? Was he, in fact, a worrier?

The simple answer was yes.

He'd started worrying about the prospect of having to make a father-of-the-bride speech while Rachel was still pregnant with Molly and a pang of concern had surfaced periodically ever since and he suspected that his own brand of anxiety was unusual.

Take his fear of flying, for instance. In the days leading up to a flight, he'd have visions of the plane plummeting to the ground or of a sudden explosion accompanied by a fleeting realisation of imminent doom, but he wouldn't feel panicky or lose sleep over it.

Yes, it was one of the worst ways to die—in public, along with dozens of desperate, hysterical people and possibly your loved ones. However, once you'd contemplated that eventuality, what else was there to go over?

The concern he felt didn't translate into panic as it had done with Rachel's fear of flying and once he was on the plane—although the awareness of imminent mass death was still there—he was able not to let it overwhelm him.

As an essentially shy person, however, most public encounters induced a certain level of anxiety, but the advantage of a date for Calum, as opposed to 'normal' social interaction, was that it was an artificial situation anyway and wouldn't just consist of small talk, which he was generally poor at. You could, he imagined, to a certain extent, cut to the chase and ask interesting questions. You were also spared the task of trying to chat someone up. For these reasons he wasn't too worried about it yet.

The mnemonic that he'd come up with to guide him through the evening had also served to reassure him. It was PLEASER, which stood for:

Positivity, **L**isten, **E**ye contact, **A**sk questions, **S**mile, **E**mpathise, **R**elax.

An alternative acronym had been RELAPSE and he actually preferred the prioritisation of points that that configuration offered, as relaxation was the foundation on which everything else was built and was also something that he'd recently discovered that he could actually control.

He'd found that all he normally had to do now before having to speak in public, for example, was to tell himself to smile and relax and to act as if he were relaxed and, miraculously, he would actually feel and come across as relaxed.

He was going to go with PLEASER, however, as it was more in keeping with the positivity that his *aide memoire* prescribed, and what's more, it had a sauciness to it that would hopefully be in keeping with some of the tone of the evening.

One thing he would need to remember, though, would be to resist the urge, after a few drinks, to reveal his cunning acronym on the date itself and thus potentially shoot himself in the foot.

Self-sabotage had been a recurring feature of Calum's social interaction over the years, particularly when inebriated or when his adrenaline was pumping. Normally rather circumspect and socially pretty self-aware (often to the point of crippling inertia), he would sometimes throw caution to the wind when alcohol had been consumed and his customary restraint could be seen for what it was—mainly inhibition.

Alcohol would therefore have to be consumed in moderation. Moderation in all things had always seemed like an immoderate amount of moderation, but it would definitely have to be the order of the day. He'd heard that some people really went for it on dates. If they liked the look of each other and got on well in the initial exchanges, they'd get straight in there with a series of shots, presumably to power through any awkwardness and accelerate the whole process. Lucky for them if they were both equally up for that approach and it all worked out.

His personal view of life was that everything was down to luck—not in the sense that every happy or 'successful' person had luck on their side rather than talent or hard work, but in the sense that the fact that some people were innately gifted or hard-working and others weren't was a matter of pre-determination based on nature and nurture that ultimately stretched all the way back to the big bang.

His thinking could best be summed up as follows: To be responsible for what you do, you have to be responsible for what you are, but to be responsible for what you are, you would have had to create yourself and, of course, that is impossible. People are, therefore, always a product of what came before them.

This also undermined the whole concept of meritocracy, as you can no more justify the advancement of the intelligent or hard-working over the intellectually-challenged or feckless than you can that of the privileged over the deprived.

Rachel had been vehemently opposed to this view of the world because the corollary was that, ultimately, nobody was responsible for their actions. That was true, of course, and Calum didn't like that aspect of it any more than she did, but as logic seemed to dictate that it was the case, he accepted it. The key for him, however, was that it didn't deny the need for boundaries of behaviour. All games need rules. The trickier issue however, was what happens to those who break the rules. Without responsibility, how can there be punishment? He was still looking for an answer to that one.

Rachel had also assumed that his view was a kind of fatalism—what will be, will be—but for him it wasn't quite the same. If a fatalist was playing chess, for example, it wouldn't matter where they moved their pieces, as the outcome, in their eyes, was already pre-ordained. Fatalistically moving your pieces at random wouldn't win you many games—unless your opponent was doing the same, in which case you'd probably win roughly fifty per cent of the time—and you would have turned chess into a foolish game of chance into the bargain.

Certain aspects of life were like a game, but life in general wasn't a game of chance—it wasn't like roulette—it was more akin to chess; there was an element of control. This control depended on our decisions, decisions which, of course, were dictated by our brains—brains that we didn't create and couldn't programme for ourselves. The control, therefore, was also beyond our control.

Our success also, ultimately, depended on the quality of our rivals; as everything was, ultimately, relative, and the mating game was, biologically-speaking, the most important game in town—a matter of life and death, the crux, the nub—but whether someone falls for you and you for them was entirely beyond your control and in fact eluded a good proportion of the population. Into this whole mix, of course, you could also toss the element of chance outcomes or encounters.

Why couldn't it just be a natural, automatic process like it is for animals, where everyone seemed to find someone? You did a little dance, you flapped your arms around, maybe turned the collar of your shirt up and—Bob's your uncle—the family line was secured.

Calum, however, wasn't approaching his impending date as if it was a game of chess—the aim of the exercise was, after all, to win her over rather than overcome her, to forge a bond—assuming, that is, that there were any sparks to work with.

What normally made him most nervous in life were situations where his personality or ability was being judged—the first few lessons with a new class, for example, or a best man's speech, and a date was basically an evening where someone sat opposite you judging your personality, behaviour and character. Curiously, however, he wasn't feeling that nervous as he got ready to go and meet this intriguing stranger thrown up by the Internet, who had agreed to spend an evening with him on a trial basis. Some people said that nerves were a good thing—the fuel that enables you to up your game, but he'd never found that. For him they were a distraction and an inhibitor.

Maybe he wasn't nervous because it was an audience of one and he tended to be better at one-to-ones. He often found that his timing was off at dinner parties and he couldn't get a word in edgeways. He'd think of something funny or interesting to say, but not be able to slip it into the micro-gaps in the conversation until it was too late. Trying to retain this spark of wit or pearl of wisdom while waiting for the moment to insert it into the conversation would also mean that he would often lose the thread of the discussion, thus making it even harder for him to chip in, or resulting in him unwittingly repeating something that someone else had already said.

The other reason that he was relatively calm was that he didn't really know what she was like and therefore had no idea of what he stood to lose by messing things up. The nerves were likely to kick in on the night, though, if he was attracted to her.

She looked great in her profile picture—intelligent eyes, attractive—and seemed to be into some of the same things as him, but, as was the case with his own picture, it probably showed her at her untypical best. He knew he wasn't to everyone's taste and could tell that some people really didn't like the cut of his jib, but he had got over that hurdle in this case.

She reminded him of someone, but he couldn't think who. Maybe he'd seen her before somewhere or she just had one of those faces.

14

Anna always felt guilty about the slight cloud of depression that she felt whenever she returned to her hometown. She'd had a happy childhood on the whole, but it always seemed slightly grubbier and tackier every time she went back. Her mother would have moved out of the town she'd been born in long ago if she'd had her way, but her dad was such a character and figure in the community that he was embedded there, and, though she'd never admit it, her mother quite enjoyed the reflected glory of being his partner. Not that she wasn't something of a character herself. She also liked the fact that people couldn't work out where he was from. They could tell he wasn't Indian or Pakistani, but he didn't seem Italian or Greek either. The more discerning presumed he was perhaps Maltese.

Sam knew everyone, had time for *mostly* everyone, and everyone knew him. They ran a hairdressing business—*S and E*— together—a merger of their originally separate salons. Sam ran the barbering side and she mainly did the ladies, though Sam didn't object to an invitation to help out there if he could. They also repaired and altered clothes, but less so as retirement approached. Anna could never see her dad hanging up his scissors—he conformed to the sad cliché that he wouldn't know what to do with himself if he retired.

Despite being hollowed out and haunted by all that they'd experienced as bereaved parents, and although they inevitably bickered from time to time, they were still the best of friends and each other's greatest admirers. The death of a child sometimes drove the parents apart, but it had brought them closer together. They were inseparable. *What therefore God hath joined together, let no man put asunder!*

She decided to walk from the station as it was only a ten-minute stroll to her parents' from there and she always liked to have a look around on her own when she could, despite the melancholy feelings it provoked. It enabled her to feel Ben's spirit again and properly feel his presence again and there was also a general bittersweet nostalgia to be experienced that she couldn't encounter anywhere else.

The sun was tentatively out and there was a brisk, heightened quality to the clouds as she walked down King Street. All the red brick made it feel like a northern outpost, but it was too far south to claim *Gateway-to-the-North* status. Despite its burgundy livery, the new Costa coffee shop looked out of place, while the barber shop of her dad's long deceased old rival, Billy Wink, still stood in dust-preserved suspended animation exactly as it had been on the day he died in 1991; with a few car and boxing magazines scattered across the seating, and unsold combs still hanging in a yellowed rack on the wall by the mirrors.

The old newsagents', Bensons, was still going strong, however, and she went in to buy a Raspberry Ruffle bar, like the ones that she and Ben would buy on their way home from school, but they didn't seem to sell them anymore so she contented herself with a Fry's Chocolate cream. The young girl behind the counter remarked on how much she herself liked them and that she hadn't had one for ages but might be treating herself to one later. The famous friendliness…

Did it feel like home? Were these her people? Did it matter? Was she proud of the place? Indifferent? Embarrassed? Defensive? At different times, *yes* would have been her answer to all of these questions, but she still wasn't sure whether it was a good thing or not to have roots in a place—to have a sense of a hometown. Was it a failing to feel it or not to feel it? The thing now, though, was that she was bound to the place by Ben. He and the town were inextricably linked—nearly all of her memories of him were caught up with the place—the sunny walks to and from school, the bonfire night they'd had to run and hide from the police, the afternoons spent listening to his U2 records when he was out.

Even though she knew it didn't matter to anyone, she was always eager to arrive at her parents' house at the time she said she would. The hedge and other bushes around the 1930s semi were looking a bit unkempt and she knew her mother would have been on at her dad to cut them back for weeks—Eileen could never understand why his enthusiasm for trimming didn't extend to foliage. Anna went along the side of the house and round the back, where the door was normally left unlocked during the day. She knocked on opening and gave a two-syllable mock call out of 'Hi' as she went in.

It was curious how the house still didn't smell of anything to her—she'd often wondered how it had smelled to her childhood friends whenever they came round, as their houses all had such distinct smells. Her brother Dan was the first to greet her before she'd got halfway across the kitchen. She sensed he was about to quickly whisper something to her, but her parents bustled in noisily behind him and he just proceeded with his embrace.

'Anna Heron, why you wear bloody scarfage around head?'

Her dad had taken to appropriating the way she and her brothers sometimes used to mimic him when they were kids.

She'd forgotten to take the tichel off.

'Oh, do you like it? I saw it in a charity shop and thought I'd give it a whirl. Do you think I can carry it off?'

'We are truly *tichel*ed to see you as always, of course, but it is shame to keep that beautiful head of hair —how you say—under wraps.'

'Don't make eye contact with him, Anna. He'll get the message eventually.'

Her mother exuded the virgin rainforest fragrance of *Eden* as usual and she enjoyed having a few strands of her hair across her face as they embraced.

'What did you do to your eye?'

'Believe it or not, I opened a door into my own face. I thought I'd told you about it?'

'No, you didn't, but actually I did that myself once. You think how the hell did that happen, don't you?'

'I tell you what though, I just seem to becoming more and more of a klutz as I get older.'

'Older schmolder', said Dan, who could never resist mocking her affected yiddishisms.

Her parents looked well and there didn't seem to be any tension in the air, so what had Dan been keen to tell her? No doubt they'd be able to steal a private moment later.

They all went through to the living room, had a cup of tea and then set off on foot to the common, which was just a few streets away.

It had clouded over again while she had been inside and a very light drizzle started to fall as they all walked along arm in arm. It was one of those drizzles that leaves a fine mist on your face and is pleasant up until the point where it starts to drip down your cheeks. Anna resolved to enjoy it while she could.

Her parents asked about Noah and work and Dan filled them in on him and his partner's progress with IVF. Things were busy for her parents at the salon and the new girl seemed to be settling in ok now after a shaky start—she was very good with the older ladies, which was not always the case with the younger ones these days.

They'd made this pilgrimage so many times now, but the pain she felt—the pain they all felt—was still keen and an air of solemnity soon settled over them.

The tree, a Black Mulberry, had been planted some eight years earlier after the original was snapped in the sapling stage by some teenagers. A sturdy but elegant, hooped metal tree guard like those seen on National Trust properties had ensured its survival and it had fruited for the first time last year.

A veil of drizzle still danced lethargically around them and as they approached, they could see that some kind of garment had been hung over the guard. As they got closer, they saw that it was a brown raincoat. Curiously, for so voluble a family, none of them mentioned it; it was just there. Her mother laid a bouquet of flowers by the plaque, which said, *This tree was planted in loving memory of Ben Aharoni 1969 – 1996.*

As was their custom on this occasion, they just stood for a little while with their heads bowed, thinking their own thoughts of their son and brother. Anna recalled the surprising weight and coarse, grainy feel of his ashes in her hand as they had each thrown a handful into the hole that the original tree was planted in. Ian had been there that first time too and had also filled up as he'd thrown a handful of her brother's remains into the earth. She'd wondered whether they were actually his ashes. Did it matter? Either way, they would never know. She looked across at her dad and recalled the sunny afternoon when he'd climbed up the apple tree in their garden and shook the boughs to make the apples fall down to Ben and her down below with their cycling helmets on, gleefully trying to catch them as they fell all around their heads, shoulders and outstretched arms.

There was still a little fruit on the tree among the elongated, heart-shaped leaves and she and her parents picked some and ate them there and then, trying to avoid getting too much of the sweet and sour, dark purple juice on their fingers.

Her mother had already gathered most of the year's fruit and again turned it into jam. Anna had delayed opening last year's jars for as long as possible to preserve it until the new supply was ready and had just about managed it. She was desperate to avoid any mould appearing, but didn't want to have to use it all up or throw any away before the next batch arrived. It was a balancing act and just the sort of private challenge that she liked to burden herself with. Maybe she'd get round to making some herself one of these days.

They tied the flowers to the bottom of the tree guard and headed back towards town. They were going to eat at the Italian rather than the Fleece. Apparently, it was under new management and was actually pretty good. As they turned into Rugby Road, Anna was just about to ask her parents why they'd chosen to plant a Mulberry tree—something she'd been meaning to do for a long while—when her dad stopped in his tracks. They followed his gaze across the street towards Coen's solicitors and saw that someone was trying to remove a large yellow star that had been painted across the window.

'What the hell! Who's done that? Bloody idiots.'

'Bloody morons. Let's not go over. They won't want people nosing and fussing around now. I'll give Jimmy a ring later.'

They walked on, their mood now even more sombre.

'Who the bloody hell has done that? They're not even Jewish anyway. They're Irish. Bloody idiots.'

'Well, it shows what level these people are operating at.'

Dan, who worked for Thames Valley police, looked up and down the street.

'There are CCTV cameras up there and they look pretty high spec so they could well be within range and have captured something'

'If they've got any sense, they'll be all hoodied up, baseball cap pulled down, head bowed.'

'Why do they hate us so much? We can never relax, can we? When will it ever end?'

'They say it never happened and yet they taunt us about it.'

'Yeah, how does that work? Explain that one to me.'

By the time they were all seated at Vernazza's, they'd managed to put it to one side. It hadn't always been just the four of them. For the first five years, Ben's fiancée, Steph, had joined them at the Fleece, but then she'd remarried and her new man hadn't approved of the exercise. So, for a couple of years she made excuses and then they eventually moved away. She did still send them a Christmas card—secretly, they presumed.

The restaurant's colour scheme was very much centred around caramel, chocolate and cream, which explained its popularity with her mum, whose nickname was the Caramel

Queen due to her fondness of the hue in both her wardrobe and home furnishings.

They ordered sparkling water and toasted Ben. She used to be tempted to say that they could drink if they wanted to, even though she really didn't want them to, but she now knew that they had long realized not only how vulnerable she was around this time, but how the beast was squatting there every day, watching, waiting—indefatigable. They understood. Her mum's uncle had drunk himself to death in the pubs and clubs of Liverpool.

Anna always wanted to make eye contact with each of them during the toast, even though she dreaded not seeing a tear in their eyes, a tear that would nevertheless ensure the welling of her own. The chink of glasses was the latest chime in an ongoing death knell. She wondered why toasts always felt empty without alcohol.

How many more of these gatherings would there be? Would Noah or her niece join them in a few years' time? Would other tragedies supersede that of Ben?

She'd dreamt about him last night, as she sometimes did, and had experienced her grief afresh on waking up to realise that he was no longer walking this earth.

She was drawn back to the present by an awareness of her mother's interrogative tone being directed towards her.

'Sorry, Mum, I was miles away. What did you say?'

'I was just saying that we liked the piece you wrote last week, but we didn't understand the bit about Nick Clegg.'

'Oh, that was the week before—I got crucified for last week's effort. The Nick Clegg thing wasn't that funny really. It was a reference to him saying that he had slept with "no more than thirty women."'

'Of course. Actually, that *is* quite funny. Did you read it, Dan?'

'Trish read some bits out to me, I think. I read all of last week's though. Pure gold.'

She was used to Dan's sarcasm about her articles—it was a sort of arrangement that they'd come to in order to avoid getting into an argument. Her parents decided to keep their own counsel on that one. They were immensely proud and protective of her success and even though privately they had serious reservations about the provocative line she took, would never voice them in public.

'I'm thinking of changing tack actually, you'll be pleased to hear.'

'Really?'

'Yes, I think I'm done with the whole revisionist history lesson schtick. I might do the odd piece if something really interesting comes up, but I think I've more or less said my piece on that front.'

Her mother noticed that Dan looked sceptically amused.

'So, what are you thinking of focusing on instead then?'

'Anything that takes my fancy really. I've still got the sport and the showbiz stuff, of course, but I'm feeling a bit overextended, to be honest.'

Her dad broke his silence.

'Yes, maybe you should give the others a go anyway. I bet they hate you, hogging all the copy.'

'People think it's a piece of cake, writing two or three articles a week. It's ok for a while, but it becomes relentless and you can start to feel stale or burnt out.'

She glanced at Dan to see if there was any hint of inner eye-rolling.

'They warned me about it, but you just feel invincible when you're young.'

'Maybe you need to think about dropping one of the columns then?'

'I know, I should really, but I've got a contract and the financial screws are very much being tightened in the industry at the moment. I'm going to speak to Sally next week and see what the options are.'

She was conscious that all the talk was about her.

'So, how are things in the land of Plod, Sergeant Aharoni?'

'Oh, you know, plodding along nicely. The seedy underbelly of Newbury is well under control.'

The waiter arrived with her and her mother's main courses and the others followed soon after. She could well understand how Italian cuisine had come to take over the planet with its unpretentious elegance. She just wished there were a few more vegetables involved.

Dan seemed slightly pissed off about something. She wondered what he had wanted to say to her earlier. It was probably something about her mum or dad. They were unlikely to get another opportunity to discuss it today, but he could always give her a ring later.

After the coffees—they were advised by her mother to pass on dessert as there were homemade scones at home—they headed out past a huge, full-wall, sepia photograph of a Tuscan landscape—hilltop village, rolling hills, cypress and olive trees scattered around—into the grey, down-market banality of small-town high-street UK.

The yellow star had gone.

Her dad and Dan walked on ahead while she and her mother stopped to look in an estate agent's window. Her mum was obsessed with property prices and it was very rare to spend a reasonable amount of time in her company without her raising the issue at some point.

Even though she never said it directly, as she knew it would be counter-productive, she was particularly keen to let Anna know about the mansions she could buy there for what she could sell her flat in London for.

'Look at this one. Late Victorian town house, four bedrooms, two bathrooms, new kitchen, huge south-facing garden, views of the river. £210,000.'

Anna knew full well what her mother's game was, but didn't want to get drawn into an argument or to give her false hopes in that direction, so she went for a mildly enthusiastic tone that was two or three levels above pointedly flat.

'Mmm, nice.'

Conscious that it might have come out a little more curt than she had intended, she added, 'Lovely fireplace.' And then tempered it with, 'A bit run-down, that area, isn't it?'

'Au contraire—up and coming. There's a very nice deli just opened.'

The pattern was repeated for another three properties before Anna had to literally drag her mother away under the guise of affectionately but firmly linking arms and drawing her off in pursuit of her dad and Dan.

To appease her, she thought about asking how much she reckoned their place was worth now, but decided against it for fear that mother might think she was just curious about her inheritance. She was also intrigued by the fact that she hadn't been sure whether to refer to it as 'your house', 'our house' or 'the house'. None of them had seemed quite right, but she plumped for 'the house' and then realized that she could have just said, 'So how much do you reckon 10 Arran would go for now?'

Getting back to the house was a predictably slow process due to all the chats that they had to stop and have with the assorted townsfolk they passed on the way. Half of them seemed to already know about the vandalism on the solicitor's window and the other half weren't sure whether, or how, to bring it up.

Once home, tea was promptly made and scones with clotted cream and Mulberry jam served. Her dad got the photo albums out. There were general ones and one for each of their children and they looked through Ben's first and lingered over the frozen moments. The process didn't feel manufactured to her—she wasn't bored or tired of it—but she sensed that Dan's heart wasn't really in it anymore and he left soon after he'd finished his cream tea, saying that he was working nights and there was something he needed to see to beforehand.

She was planning to get back to Euston for half past six. Noah was going round to a friend's for tea, but she didn't want to leave him round there for too long. She missed him during the day and if she didn't get to spend a decent amount of time with him before bedtime, she felt as if she hadn't had a proper evening.

Her parents understood and didn't make her feel like she was rushing off. Her dad gave her a lift back to the station and took the opportunity to reassure her that she didn't need to change anything for their sake, that she just needed to focus on herself and Noah and they would support any decision she made about her career and Noah's upbringing.

On the train, she tried to get some work done but couldn't concentrate as she was aware of an edgy-looking man with a tinny, frenetic dance beat leaking out of his headphones sitting across the aisle eyeing her with a hostile gleam in his eye. He had a defiant can of lager in his hand—the second of a four-pack ranged in front of him. When he'd finished the can off with what he took to be a manly flourish, he immediately hissed open another and took another long swig. As was often the case in situations where she came across objectionable people, she reminded herself of what her father had once said about most of us having had a hard road to travel down one way or another and that you don't know what people have been through. *Hurt people hurt people.* So, just before the next stop, she nonchalantly got up and moved to another carriage and found an unreserved seat. No longer feeling in the mood to do any work, she put her earphones in and quietly listened to Radio 4 on her phone while sullenly staring out of the window at the darkening blandscapes careering past. They careened past like slides in a hectic but dreary slideshow, interspersed with stark flashes of her own reflection as they passed under bridges.

9

Calum had set off early, even though he knew that it was pretty much accepted that it was a woman's prerogative to arrive late for dates. He was starting to feel quite nervous so he picked up a free newspaper to read on the Tube to take his mind off his anxiety. Apparently, Druidry had been recognized as a religion for the first time in the UK and the new Equality Act signalled the death knell for the office joke. He could hang on to it and read it in the pub if he ended up having to wait a while and then make a jokey, disparaging reference to it when she arrived, to test the waters of her politics.

His main concern was to make sure that she wouldn't be sitting there on her own, but he also didn't want to risk it looking like he was playing a power game or was the sort of thoughtless, disorganized person who would keep someone waiting on a date thinking that they might have been stood up.

As it turned out, however, he bumped into an old colleague from his time in Brazil outside the Tube station and had to stop to chat for almost ten minutes before it was polite to leave. This meant that he had to jog most of the seven hundred and fifty yards or so to the Mermaid in order to reach the pub on time, albeit slightly sweaty and out of breath.

As he was about to cross the road, he saw her arrive ahead of him and slip in through the main entrance. She seemed to be limping slightly.

He knew it was her, even though she was in profile and her hair was in a different style to her photo. Taking a deep breath through flared nostrils, he said, *This is it* to himself and followed her in. Wondering whether he'd need to face the awkwardness of having to tap her on the shoulder to introduce himself, he was relieved to see her veer off towards the loos straight away. A wise move. He went and positioned himself at the bar and ordered a drink.

He'd put a fair amount of thought into what he should drink. As he saw it, there were four main options:

1. Be natural and drink what he'd normally drink, i.e., Guinness or bitter.
   The advantage of this was that it was unpretentious, but the drawback was that it wasn't an inclusive choice and made an uncompromisingly manly statement. It also seemed unsophisticated and didn't conjure up the prospect of a fun or special evening.
2. Order a cocktail, hoping that it was her preferred option too—though it didn't matter if it wasn't. The question then was, which cocktail? A G+T would be a safe bet. Was that actually a cocktail though? Did it matter?
   Or perhaps something more unusual? A British Royale? The trouble with that was that there was a risk that they wouldn't know how to make it at the bar. He could look up all the ingredients, but that would make him seem a bit high-maintenance— especially if it turned out that they didn't have all of them.
3. A bottle of champagne. This option would show spontaneity, largesse and joie de vivre, but it didn't feel like him at all and could smack of desperation and maybe even coercion? Plus, it was a bit over the top for a pub.
   The other option was to wait and see what she'd like to drink and fit in with her.

Although that would help to generate complicity between them and make him seem open and easy-going, it could be construed as wishy-washy weakness and an over-eagerness to please. Maybe it was rude to just go ahead and order a drink or was it strange to do otherwise? What would a normal person do? Order first, he reckoned.

He ordered a gin and tonic. It seemed the best option, all things considered—it normally gave you a bit of a lift, didn't get you too drunk and could easily be followed by a range of other drinks— it never seemed to react badly with either beer or wine.

He considered engaging in a bit of chit-chat with the barman to get his social juices flowing before she appeared, but thought better of it when it occurred to him that the awkwardness that would probably ensue might actually damage his confidence rather than boost it. He had a tendency to slightly defer to bar and restaurant staff and treat them as if they were the ones in control of the situation. This was preferable to the other extreme of treating them as if they were your personal assistants for the evening, but he would have liked to be able to achieve some sort of equilibrium in these situations.

His drink arrived and, taking a large sip, he congratulated himself on having made the correct choice in terms of pure alcoholic refreshment. Before he knew it, he was halfway down the glass. What the hell was she doing in there? It must have been about ten minutes by now. Maybe she'd emerged without him noticing, had had second thoughts and left via a fire exit or back door? More likely, there was a queue in there or she'd bumped into someone she knew or something.

Just as he was starting to think that she'd definitely pressed the ejector seat prior to take-off, she appeared in the crowd over to his right. She looked both familiar and completely new to him at the same time.

As she approached, he could see the soul of the city in her eyes: the cool, the danger, the excitement. He tried to gauge if there was a glimmer of interest or attraction there, but all he could detect was a genial and slightly ironic detachment.

A sheet of electricity flashed through his core as her eyes briefly met his. A fathomless and timeless feeling tore through his chest. It was as if a subconscious prophecy underpinning his whole existence was being fulfilled.

He remembered to kiss the right cheek first, as his instinct was always to kiss the left—he still didn't feel entirely comfortable with the twin air kiss greeting, but was getting more used to it. It seemed to suit the Latin male pretty well, but he still struggled to pull it off without it feeling awkward and affected.

Fortunately, this embrace passed off relatively smoothly. She smelled great and, as the G+T was already taking effect, he told her so. He wasn't a connoisseur of fragrances, so couldn't impress her by identifying it, but she may not have been impressed by that sort of thing anyway.

She accepted his offer of a drink and he was both impressed and slightly embarrassed when she ordered a pint of Guinness. She had a husky catch in her voice.

When her pint arrived, he felt rather effete with his Gin and tonic in a balloon glass.

As they looked round for somewhere to sit, he saw the actor Jason Isaacs sitting with a friend over by the fireplace. He didn't think she'd noticed but he decided not to mention it as he didn't want it to seem like he was the sort of person for whom it was a big deal. He might casually mention it later if there was a lull in the conversation.

He followed her over to a table round a corner by the window. She had shoulder-length hair, the colour of dark chocolate. *Brown hair is sweet. Brown hair across the mouth blown.* They took their coats off and sat down.

Her eyes were an arresting sea blue. She also had slightly laterally crooked front teeth, which he, for some reason, had always found attractive.

One thing that had drawn him to her profile was that she had stipulated that '*bad boys and cheeky chappies need not apply*' and, in the flesh, she had a slightly, intimidating, no-nonsense air about her—a shrewd, observant look in her eye. She was definitely out of his league, but the fact that there was something familiar about her gave him confidence. He felt as if he was in a waking dream or on the threshold of a portal into another world.

'My voice doesn't always sound this sexy, I'm afraid—I've had a bit of a cold. I thought I might have to cancel this morning actually.'

Was it too early in the proceedings to say, '*I'm glad you didn't*'?

'Well, I'm glad you didn't.'

She raised her eyebrows and turned her head slightly, as if to say, *That's a bit much, at this stage, wouldn't you say?*

She had an archness about her, which he objectively approved of, but knew would keep him very much on his toes the whole time. He felt like he was in the presence of a film star. She also had the flat vowels and slightly deeper-toned voice that northern women often had. He decided to just get stuck in with the questions.

'Where are you from then? You sound a like you might be of the northern persuasion.'

'Well, we moved around a bit when I was young, but basically from the north, yes. What about you?'

He'd described where he was from in various ways over the years, because, if he was honest, he wasn't sure where he *was* from exactly. His parents were from one county, he'd been born in another and then his parents had moved back to a different part of their home county when he was at primary school. To complicate matters further, his parents' hometown had since then been mysteriously shunted into a neighbouring county. Also, curiously, the longer he'd lived in London, the less northern he'd become, but the more northern he'd felt.

'Lancashire,' he said.

'Ah, you must be on tenterhooks now, wondering which side of the Pennines it's going to be for me then.'

'Au contraire, it's obviously neither here nor there…'

'Well, I was born in Cumbria and that's where all my family are from.'

'I love the Lakes.'

'Me too—so many people down here have never been, though—but it's not really the Lakes. It's Barrow.'

He was quietly pleased with this development as it meant she wouldn't be able to lord it over him geographically or demographically. He chose to be diplomatic, though.

'I've been there once—to a rugby match. I didn't really see much of the place.'

He fleetingly wondered if he should point out that Barrow used to be in Lancashire, but decided that it hardly constituted sparkling banter.

'It's not exactly Venice, to be honest, but naturally, I'm defensive of it if anyone starts slagging it off. We're not actually from Barrow itself though—just outside, and we moved down to Lancashire when I was eight anyway. My grandparents still live up there, though, near Coniston.'

He imagined a handsome, converted stone farmhouse with a Scandinavian style wood-and-exposed-stone interior and a real fire burning in the hearth.

She didn't seem impatient to move the conversation on from matters geographical, which was a good sign for him.

He asked some questions—not too many, he hoped—listened (almost all of the time) to what she said and managed to make plenty of eye contact—hopefully, not in too creepy a way.

Normally, Calum had to stop himself from being a bit on the serious side and potentially boring with people he didn't know very well, and if he did make any attempts at humour, they tended to veer towards puns. In his experience, women usually found wordplay tedious, but when he warned her in advance about this tendency, she said, 'Don't worry, I won't necessarily have you dragged off to the *pun*ishment block if you go down that route. I'm a writer—wordplay has its place. It's all about the quality.'

He tried to get her to talk about her writing, but she seemed reluctant to go into much detail. She did reveal, however, that in her mid-twenties she'd done a bit of TEFL in Italy and Portugal. He talked about his time in France and Brazil, the general joys of TEFL and then they'd tried to outdo each other with the crappy jobs they'd done before that.

They laughed at how a date could easily feel like a two-way job interview if you weren't careful and then they swapped a few of their best interview stories.

The conversation then turned to their schooldays and she revealed how she'd been bullied because of her weight.

He was about to say, *Really? That's hard to believe— you look amazing now*, but instead responded with, 'That must have been awful. There was hardly any work done in schools on bullying back then. It was pretty much a free-for-all. I think a lot of kids didn't even realize that they *were* bullying—it was so ingrained.'

'It was pretty bad for several years, but I survived. The worst thing was you'd hear people stage-whispering, "It's such a shame she's so chubby; you can see she's got a really pretty face. If only she could lose some weight..." Were you bullied at school?'

'Not that I can remember. I got into a few scraps with older lads, but I wouldn't say it was because I was being bullied. You got the piss taken out of you by your mates or the older kids if you'd had a bad haircut or were wearing some naff shoes your parents had made you wear or something. I had bad acne and was self-conscious about it, but actually, when I think about it now, I don't remember anyone even mentioning it—I don't think I got called pizza face or anything like that. Maybe it was so bad that it was beyond ridicule! It did really dent my confidence at the time though—especially with girls. It also makes you feel unlucky that you've got it and most other kids haven't at a time when you're really self-conscious about your looks anyway and oversensitive about what others think of you.'

He thought about mentioning that his mother had probably given him more of a complex about it than necessary by taking him to the doctors, where he was prescribed Retin-A, which dried his face out and made him look like a powdery pale Queen Bess, but decided that he'd probably gone on about his situation too much and needed to find out more about what she'd been through. He remembered to make eye contact with her again and also consciously properly noticed her lips for the first time —she didn't seem to be wearing lipstick and her lips had a natural pastel pinkness to them that was like the interior of a seashell.

'How did you cope with it all then—the bullying—at the time?' *Shit. She'd already talked about that.*

'It wasn't great, but it could have been worse. Adolescence is a tunnel for a lot of kids, isn't it? My mum, who was a teacher, used to say that you need to see your teen years as a bridge, not a tunnel, but for me it was definitely more of a tunnel. When you're that age, you're so wrapped up in the here and now that it doesn't feel like just a phase or a step towards something else. It feels like the be all and end all. And, as a teenager, you feel like you are very much the raw, cutting edge of humanity.'

'True. I like "*the raw, cutting edge of humanity*," by the way. Is it one of your lines?'

'I think so, but, then again, I could have picked it up from somewhere.'

He decided to try and broach the topic of her writing again.

'What sort of stuff do you write then?'

'A bit of this and a bit of that, but I mainly specialise in semi-fiction.'

'And you're making a decent living out of it?'

'I get by.'

'I should probably have heard of you, shouldn't I?'

'Oh, you definitely should. I'm the doyenne of North London bohemia. My salon is the stuff of legend.'

'Well, I'm very impressed. Writing a novel's such a difficult thing to pull off. Then you've got to get it published and hope people buy it. I had a cursory go in my twenties, but found it really hard to properly get down to it and see it through. I still pretentiously keep a notebook that I jot odd ideas and phrases down in when I remember to, but it doesn't feel as if it's leading anywhere in particular. I really admire someone who can actually pull the whole thing off. *Chapeau bas, madame*.'

'Merci.'

'I did manage to write a short personal empowerment book though.'

'Oh, yes?'

'It's called, '*How to think for yourself.*'

'Boom boom!'

'I'll get my coat.'

He considered mentioning the poetry that he'd penned too, but decided against it.

'I was also in a bit of a band around that time and that took over for a while.'

'*A bit of a band,* you say?'

'It was just a glorified bedroom band, really.'

'Well, if you weren't in a band back then, there was something wrong with you. What sort of music was it?'

'Sort of jangly, soul-indie. As you can imagine, we spent many a long hour coming up with that term at the time. I was into Van Morrison and the Smiths, amongst other things, so it was a bit of an odd combo—Van Morrissey, if you will.'

'Now, that would be an intriguing tribute band... It wasn't your actual name, though, was it?'

'Hah. No. We were called Resistance.'

'Ooh, edgy, but dangerous, methinks, as it invites the review headline, *RESISTANCE ARE USELESS.*'

'We actually did get that very headline for our only proper gig in Manchester! It wasn't you that wrote it, was it?'

She laughed, 'You know, it could well have been. I was in music journalism for a while and travelled round the country a bit. Where was the gig?'

'The Magpie.'

'One for sorrow... Could well have been me. I saw lots of up-and-coming bands and was scathing about most of them. That was my schtick.'

She put a finger to her lips and mused archly.

'I'm just trying to think of any spotty, gladioli-laden white soul men I might have come across... So what happened to the band then—the old cliché; musical differences?'

'More or less. We never properly got off the ground. We made a demo and did a few little gigs but it didn't feel right. I think we all got started a bit too late. Were you ever in a band then? Or do you play any instruments or anything? You're obviously into music…'

'I did my grade one piano and I "guest-vocalled" a couple of times with a band called O at sixth form, but not much else to write home about. Another band name that was a gift for the critics, I hear you say…You're being very good with the questions, by the way.'

'Why thank you. It's just second nature with me and not at all pre-conceived.'

'I've had long conversations with men—and a few women, to be fair—where they literally didn't ask me a single thing. By the end of the conversation, you know everything about them—their parents' divorce, their in-laws, their kids' recent homework, when their dog died etc.—but they know absolutely nothing about you. How can you reach our age and be so oblivious? And these are people in high-powered jobs, where people skills are meant to be key!'

'It's not rocket science, is it?'

'Ooh, I hate that phrase.'

'Me too, actually. What did we used to say before the space age? Anyway, another question… Have you been on many dates then?'

'Quite a few, to be honest. I actually wrote a book about it.'

'Comedy or tragedy?'

'A bit of both.'

'I'm sorry, I should probably have heard of it, but I'm not really up on contemporary fiction. I wasn't much of a reader when I was a kid and I'm still trying to catch up on all the old stuff. I'm not unwittingly sitting opposite one of the literary greats of our time, am I?'

'I'm doing OK, but I'm not Isabelle Allende or anything.'

'I would have googled you, but I don't know your surname.'

'I use another name anyway.'

'You're not John le Carré are you?'

'No, I'm actually Thomas Pynchon.'

'Ah. Cunning to make us all think that you're American… On the subject of pseudonyms… You know how in the past female writers sometimes used a male pseudonym? Are you aware of any male writers who have a female nom de plume?'

She looked slightly askance and he thought that he might be treading on dodgy ground, but he pressed on nevertheless.

'It seems to me that things have been turned upside down since George Eliot's day and that it might be more of an advantage to be a female writer these days, seeing that most readers are female and generally seem to read more books written by women than men do. Aren't most of the best-selling authors of the last one hundred years or so all women? JK Rowling, Agatha Christie, Enid Blyton?'

'You seem quite au fait with modern literary trends after all… Let's just say that I think that some of the old prejudices remain and I can neither confirm nor deny whether John Grisham is a willowy, hippy divorceé living in Hebden Bridge, Yorkshire.'

'I suspected as much. So what's your pen name?'

'Maria Cormack. Not very exotic, I know, but it's a mash-up, as the kids say— or not, as the case may be—of my parents' surnames.'

'Cunning. Anyway, let's get back to your dating project.'

'What makes you think it was a project?'

'I dunno. Didn't you say it was? '

'I don't believe so. Anyway, I was just going on a lot of bad dates to start with, but it did, in fact, turn into a kind of project. I was actually welcoming the bozos by the end.'

'It didn't put you off dating then?'

'It did for a good while and it got trickier as I became a bit better known, but I thought I'd give it another go. What about you? You've obviously been on quite a few…'

'Flattered I'm sure… but this is actually my first "proper" date—through a site. There was a stage in the early days with my ex when we first met and were still in the friend zone when we went out with another couple a few times and went to the cinema on our own once, I think, but it was ambiguous and we were still feeling each other out. Proper dating seems like a very unnatural way to meet people, but a necessary evil, I suppose and it does actually seem to work for some people.'

'We live in an unnatural world. It's like getting a job—you don't just expect to bump into someone and get offered one. You have to apply and go to interviews. There's a market and you need to advertise yourself and recruit. For some people it just doesn't happen in the normal course of life—especially if you're knocking on a bit…'

'Well, you're younger than me…'

'My birthday's in a couple of months though…'

'So, what about your previous relationships?'

'There haven't been many—just two major ones. I messed the first one up after four years and then I got messed around in the second after six, but it ended up kind of mutual and amicable in the end. Strangely, I miss the first one more. I could imagine having kids with him now, but I wasn't ready for all that back then. I was only in my early twenties.'

'So you don't have kids then?'

'No, it hasn't happened yet. You have two daughters then? How old are they?'

'Doctor's ten and Professor's going to be eight in two weeks.'

The way she had raised her eyebrows, tucked in her chin and given him the knowing look that you might give a child who is outrageously fibbing told him she wasn't falling for that hilarious jape, so he added,

'Doctor and Professor Roche. Some people might see it as mean, but we just wanted to give them a harmless leg up. It's Doc and Prof for short.'

A less indulgent version of the look was sent his way.

'Sorry. Molly's ten and Rebecca's eight. They're both great kids—I'm biased of course, but I feel very lucky. The split and divorce doesn't seem to have affected them too much so far—touch wood. They're both big readers as well. They tear through them—they put me to shame. Are you into kids? Have you got nieces or nephews or anything?'

'I've got two nieces and a nephew and they're all great. I generally love kids—as with anything else, you come across some awful ones of course. Don't feel that you need to be the one asking questions all the time, by the way. I've got a few of my own actually…'

'OK, fair enough. I'll bow to your superior dating experience.'

'I remember one of the dates, who turned out to be quite an eminent barrister, suggested a wild-card option whereby you can both ask each other a question a propos of nothing. Of course, the person suggesting it has obviously already prepared a killer random question, but it's interesting to see what the other person comes up with on the spot. It can also be quite telling what the prepared question is, too.'

'OK, fire away. What's your killer question then?'

'What does the phrase "a stick of Spanish" mean to you?'

'OK, good question—very probing, I can tell you were in journalism.'

'Thank you.'

'Well, coming from where I do, I can confidently inform you that it's a thinnish, six-inch or so rod of liquorice.'

'And as an English teacher of some standing, you'd be happy to spell *liquorice* for me, wouldn't you?'

'Very happy—deliriously happy.'

'Good. That was a joke question, by the way. For my actual question I'm torn between *What's the worst thing you've ever done*? and *What's your favourite fish?*'

116

'Do I get to choose?'

'Nope. And I think I'll… go for… the… former.'

'Mm, so many unsavoury incidents to choose from…'

Obviously, he couldn't tell her the actual worst thing—his dark secret—so he quickly sifted through for something of an acceptable level of heinousness or something amusing that might enable him to deflect the question.

'Well, as I said, I got into quite a few scraps in my youth. You know, rolling around on the pavement outside a nightclub—that sort of dignified thing. I was touchy and had low self-esteem and if someone took the piss after I'd had a fair amount to drink, I'd sometimes react.'

He expected her to look disgusted and appalled, but she was still coolly assessing him.

'It's something I've had to work on and grow out of, I suppose. Once I left uni, I seemed to keep it under wraps. This is no excuse—I'm just trying to explain the background—but when I was a kid, my dad actively encouraged fighting. If a brawl broke out in a rugby match on telly, he'd excitedly call me down to watch it as if it was the highlight of the game. And I remember coming home one evening having been in a losing fight with an older lad—Gary Hughes—when I was about twelve and my dad urged me to get back out there and finish it off. Gary had been banging my head against the kerb at one point. I think I had three fights with him in all.'

'Kids' fights are bad enough, but seeing grown men fighting is just sickening and ridiculous and you can never condone it, unless it's genuine self-defence, of course. Do you still have anger management issues then?'

'Yeah, occasionally, but they don't translate into violence anymore. Most people see me as calm and patient and are really surprised when they hear about my temper. The thing you learn is that you can stop yourself lighting the fuse by anticipating a potential situation and just telling yourself to stay serene, to rise above and not get sucked into losing it. It also really helped me get it into perspective when I learned from some of my Japanese and Korean students that anger is seen as a mark of stupidity in their culture. An idiotic loss of control.'

He thought it was time to turn the focus back on her.

'What length of fuse would you say you had?'

'Pretty long—long enough to hang myself with sometimes, probably.'

'Well, ultimately, that's what I'm doing with my short fuse too. Or maybe blowing myself up would be a better way of putting it. The difference being, though, that I'm blowing up the people around me too—*you're* the only casualty of your approach.'

'Anyway, it's time for *your* wild card question.'

'Ok. What's your favourite fish?'

She smiled. 'Without hesitation, the seahorse.'

'Good choice. Are seahorses actually fish, though?'

'Er—*yes*! What else would they be?'

'I dunno. Crustaceans? Aren't they related to shrimp or prawns?'

'Nope. Prawns have legs. Seahorses don't. They're definitely fish. Atypical, as they swim vertically, don't have scales or a tail fin, but fish nonetheless. Look it up, sunshine.'

'It's ok. I'll take your word for it. I must have been sick the day we covered all that in school. Come to think of it, I must have missed quite a few biology lessons as I also remember getting caught out when I was in Brazil, trying to give a definition of the word *mammal* to a class.'

'Ooh, I like the sound of this. Come on, out with it. What was your definition then?'

'Well, to be honest, at that early stage of my illustrious career, I'd never really thought about what makes a mammal a mammal and I'd dropped biology in the third year.'

'The excuses, the excuses…'

'So, the word *mammal* comes up and this Brazilian teenager—let's call him Pedro— doesn't understand it and asks me what it means. So, I ponder briefly and start to say that it's an animal that has bones, but then immediately fish spring to mind and, seeing the consternation on some of the students' faces, I say something along the lines of it being animals with "*proper bones—big bones.*" In the meantime, I can hear one of the kids whispering to a neighbour something about *leite,* the Portuguese word for milk, and the penny drops and, blushing to the gills, I finally give the correct definition.'

'Bravo! I *am* tempted to check your definition now, though, just for the record … No, actually, I think you should get an extra free question as I had a chance to prepare mine and you used my back-up question, anyway. as yours.'

'OK, that seems fair. Mmm… OK. What's your favourite bird?'

'Easy again — the kingfisher.'

'Another excellent choice, might I say. Your taste in matters fish and fowl is impeccable. I've always wanted to see a kingfisher and never have.'

'Well, I know a place not that far from here where you're guaranteed to see one, if you're particularly observant.'

'Oh yes. Pray tell.'

'On a quiet stretch of the River Lee slash Lee Navigation, there's a perch on one of the shaded banks where I have oftentimes seen sit a beautiful, perfectly still, electric-blue, cyan, orange and white *Alcedo atthis*. There is only one catch…'

'Don't tell me—he's made of plastic.'

'Don't be ridiculous! …Wood! Finest English oak, I believe, and exquisitely painted to unparalleled levels of verisimilitude. No, seriously, it is very lifelike and you can actually see real kingfishers along there if you're lucky.'

'Have you seen one there then?'

'Just the once and I had to get up at the crack of Ms. French for the privilege, but it was definitely worth it.'

'Well, I'm very jealous.' He stood up a bit too abruptly, sending his chair screeching backwards. 'I'm just going the loo. Do you want another drink?'

'Yes, please. I'll have a Jameson. A double, on ice please.'

This boded well—it looked like she might be going for it.

'Wow, you're a rum one with your Guinness and Jameson's.'

'Not so much rum... Dating's a *whisky* business for a girl.'

'It might be *me* dragging *you* off to the *pun*ishment block if you're not careful... I prefer a *rye* sense of humour myself.'

He was a bit more eager to get to the toilet than he'd let on, as an ever-expanding urge to pass wind was putting extra pressure on his bladder. On the way, he also had to wait for a guy to finish throwing his darts in order to get to the loo. Bit of a stupid place to put the board. The bloke missed the double 4 he was after.

He was bursting by the time he got in. In these situations, he'd found that he couldn't start to pee until the wind had been released, but unfortunately, there was someone else at the urinals and the sole cubicle was occupied.

He therefore stood at the urinal conspicuously and self-consciously, not producing anything alongside a free-flowing stranger, who was in resounding mid-micturition.

Someone had scrawled, *The answer to the question of life, the universe and everything is... 42* on the wall to the right of him so, still not peeing, he overtly focused on that and was soon distracted by the thought that, actually it wasn't, it was O. It was everything and nothing, a shape, a number, a letter and a word. Old Dougie had missed a trick. On second thoughts, maybe not... 42 was funnier.

Mercifully, his urinarily equine neighbour briefly, but vigorously, shook himself off and left without washing his hands.

There was still the person in the cubicle to consider, but he calculated from the activity audible there that the occupant was still some way from completing his task and that it was therefore safe for him to simultaneously relax his bowels, relieve his bladder and get out of there with his anonymity intact.

The gods of scatology were clearly on his side, however, as, at that precise moment, a crescendo of doppling sounds from the cubicle drowned out both the sound and odour of his own emissions.

A most fortuitous cacaphony, he mused as he swiftly finished off, washed his hands and went to the drier. He wondered if he'd actually said it out loud— he didn't think he had—and the initial pleasure at this Joycean neologism faded as he reflected on whether it was desirable to be turning into Leopold Bloom at his age anyway.

When he emerged from the loo, the same dartsman had just landed a bull and was celebrating winning Round the Board as Calum slipped behind him without breaking a step as the victor went to retrieve his darts.

Once at the bar, he started to assess how the date was going. She was quite difficult to make out and unlike any woman he'd met before, but he really liked her. There was definitely something familiar about her, though. He didn't think he'd seen her picture in the papers or whatever—it felt more like when you see someone that you've dreamed about the night before or the sense of familiarity you get in the presence of a great work of art. He felt like he'd seen her quite recently, but couldn't think where. There was also the hint of something deeper and older. Then he remembered the woman on the Tube the other day who'd smiled at him—*Rive Gauche.* She looked different with make-up on and without the beret. *Well, well, well…* He wondered if she remembered him and wasn't letting on? She'd obviously chosen a picture for the dating site that made her look plainer than she really was. She reminded him of Ava Gardner—the same softly cleft chin. When you saw her in the flesh, it was like having the window of your heart kicked in.

He didn't feel the need to run through the PLEASER checklist, as he'd been mentally ticking the boxes as he'd gone along. He'd expected to be nervous with someone he was this attracted to, but he felt that, somehow, he'd got into a groove of empathetic insouciance. Normally, he'd only find it easy to flirt with someone he didn't fancy. Was he overdoing the archness thing though?

He became aware of a familiar song playing over the pub speakers:

I was thinking about turquoise,
I was thinking about gold
I was thinking about diamonds and the world's biggest necklace.
As we rode through the canyons,
through the devilish cold,
I was thinking about Isis,
how she thought I was so reckless.

He dared to venture a half-look over at her, but she was tucked round the corner, of course, and now, as he thought of her, he realized that he was foolishly already getting romantically locked in, but even so, he felt strangely calm and almost guided.

Should he mention that he thought he'd seen her on the Tube the other day? Would that seem weird?

As the Guinness that he'd opted for was placed on pause for two minutes to contemplate its impending topping off, he gazed into the mirrored bottlescape of spirits on the shelf behind the bar, savouring the international glamour of the names—Martell, Cardhu, Curaçao, Amaretti, Yamazaki—each label, shape of bottle and colour of glass offering the promise of a different milieu of sophistication and experience.

Turning, as if in slow motion, he observed the *amorous, vinous* light of a bar lamp refracted in a glass of red wine along the bar. It was one of those rare moments when he felt entirely happy in his skin—past, present and future all one, as the centre of the universe slowly wheeled across him.

He turned back to the bar and saw a tired and slightly wild-eyed face in the mirrored wall behind the shelves of spirits, realised it was his own and, as would sometimes happen in these situations, when he was aware of being happy and things going right, a voice whispered in his head, *'None of this matters. It's all meaningless. You're not going to feel anything. It's not going to mean anything to you.'*

The Guinness was lightly hooved onto the walnut bar by the barman and rested beside the iced warmth of the Jameson. He slowly blinked and gave an almost perceptible interior shake of the head as if to delete the thought, then picked up both drinks and turned to make his way back to their table.

The pint of Guinness was a thing of everyday beauty—a stirring, dark and mysterious underworld topped off by a field of summer barley. In its simplicity and power, he told himself, it was the aesthetic equal of anything any gallery or museum had to offer. The Jameson glowed expectantly by its side.

As he rounded the corner to their snug, he saw that she wasn't there—she must have gone to the loo. Her coat had gone too though—his was still there on the back of the chair.

Maybe it was an expensive one and she didn't want to risk it being stolen. He sat down and waited.

What must have been ten minutes passed and he wondered if he should go to the ladies and get someone to check she was there, to see she was alright.

She could also be on the phone to someone—maybe she'd agreed to check in with a friend to let them know she was ok and tell them how it was going?

She might even be outside talking on the phone, as it had got pretty noisy in the pub. It could even be an emergency. How long should he leave it before checking?

He couldn't phone her or text her as he didn't have her number and it would probably seem insecure and needy at this stage anyway. It must be an urgent phone call, he told himself. He'd give her another five minutes. Was she a smoker? It might just be a case of a fag and a phone call.

She didn't seem like a smoker. You could usually tell—a kind of edginess, and a sallowness to the complexion. More like an ex-smoker perhaps. Probably not—too smart to have even started. You never know. Maybe the torment of the date had caused her to lapse…?

Five more minutes passed and he popped outside to see if she was there. She wasn't. Then he loitered by the ladies and asked the first person to come out if there was a tallish, dark-haired woman in her late thirties in there as he was worried about his friend who'd gone in about a quarter an hour ago.

She was pretty sure that there was nobody else in there, but was reluctantly persuaded to go back and check the other cubicles.

There was no one there.

'She must have escaped out of the window, love.'

He went back to his table, took a large draught of Guinness and sent her a message on the dating app.

'Is everything OK? Where are you?'

He asked the people at the next table if they'd seen her leave. They hadn't. Another five or ten minutes passed. Nothing.

The only sensible explanation was that she had bailed. It had seemed to be going so well… He felt as if he'd burst through the usual impenetrable membrane and was really connecting with her. How could he have misread it so badly?

But when he thought about it, why would she be interested in him? What did he have to offer? She was out of his league; he was basically a time waster. He couldn't blame her really. She could have been a little less brutal about it, though.

It then crossed his mind whether he should report her missing if he hadn't heard anything by the end of the evening. But that was ridiculous. The police would just assume that she'd blown him out.

'*Happens quite a lot, I'm afraid, sir.*'

She didn't seem like the sort of person who would just do a bunk like that. She'd be honest if she thought it wasn't going to go anywhere. She easily had the skills to manoeuvre him into the friend zone. Could his radar be that far off? Was he that awful?

Still no message.

She must have just been humouring him, lulling him into a false sense of security and biding her time until she could make her getaway.

He downed the Jameson and headed out into the street, where the softness of early autumn Indian summer evening languor was broken by the occasional burst of laughter.

He passed an empty kebab house, where an assistant unconvincingly busied himself under the stark, soulless strip lighting like a surgeon waiting for the patient to arrive on the operating table, the tumescent, flayed todger of meat slowly rotating in the orange glow of the grill.

Two young women who'd come out of the pub just before him were engaged in excited chatter about Jason Isaacs as they trotted ahead of him in black tights and high heels with their arms folded against the ghost of the cold.

He vaguely wondered what it was that made that look and sound so alluring.

He looked at the time on the watch that Rachel had bought him all those years ago and noticed that the little crocodile's customary air of defiance had turned to disdain. Ten past ten.

He passed by a chestnut tree overhanging the pavement and spotted a conker on the pavement just ahead of him that had come out of its case. He wanted to pick it up and feel its virgin smoothness in his hand. He could hear footsteps behind him and hesitated for a second before bending down and picking it up, almost without breaking his stride. He looked at it in the light of a shop window as he walked along. It was fresh and pristine and felt like a globule of wood polished to perfection. He manoeuvred it around the palm of his hand with his fingers, feeling its cool, natural gloss and then put it in his pocket. It reminded him of simpler times, of times when he hadn't noticed how beautiful a freshly uncased conker could be.

He got the bus home and watched the melancholic majesty of a lonely London Friday night slide by.

12

As Maria hurried along Bell Street, she instinctively glanced at her phone again even though she knew it was out of charge. She would charge it on the way up—if she could find the bloody charger. Lucky that she'd only had one drink.

Her mum seemed fairly calm before they'd got cut off, but of course she wouldn't want her to be driving up in floods of tears, so it was hard to know. Her underlying instinct was that he'd be alright, that it was just another scare, but then she'd veer to imagining that this was it and she'd get there too late. She worshipped her dad. No other man came near.

Talk about timing though. This really put the cat among the pigeons. You couldn't make it up. She was tempted to wish she had thought of something like this, but guilt soon beat those thoughts back down.

Had she absolutely needed to rush off like that? She could have gone back inside the pub after her phone died and waited a bit longer, but something just compelled her to leave there and then. Maybe that wasn't such a bad thing.

She could tell that he sort of recognized her from somewhere, but it was almost certainly just the Tube. Or that he'd unconsciously seen her photo somewhere.

He had no idea who she was. No idea at all—that was obvious. She'd thought about going for a sort of punky look and wearing their old school tie with a white shirt, but maybe even that wouldn't have made the penny drop.

She hadn't had a clear plan for the big reveal, as she didn't know whether he would already have more or less worked out who she was before the date or how far into the conversation it might finally dawn on him. Part of her couldn't help feeling disappointed that he hadn't realised it was her, as she'd hoped that, deep down, there might have been some latent affinity on his part that would be rekindled when they met.

What if he couldn't even remember who she was? Surely not—they were in the same classes for more or less ten years. She could still remember everybody's name in their primary school class.

He had only spoken to her on three occasions in all that time, though, and she could still remember each one distinctly. Boys and girls lived very much parallel lives in Yewton back then—there wasn't much interaction, on the whole, apart from at the monthly disco in the church hall and the odd party, and people didn't really turn up for the conversation.

She could tell he was keen now though. Unmistakably. But keen in what way? Imagine if she'd blown it?

In one sense, it couldn't have gone any better. The whole thing was a bit surreal, but the conversation had flowed and they did seem to be on a similar wavelength. She'd been right about the teacher thing. She and Anne-Marie had speculated that he'd ended up in South America or somewhere, living the life of a bohemian writer while involved in slightly dodgy and dangerous things, when in fact he was a divorced father of two scratching a living out of TEFL. He had lived in South America at least and given writing a bit of a go, too. Anne-Marie would be dying to find out how she'd got on…

What had he imagined had happened, she wondered? All sorts of theories must have gone through his mind.

He kind of reminded her of her dad in a funny way, although, on the face of it, they were quite different. He was essentially a sensitive soul with a bit of a hard edge that could appear from nowhere, like a harmless looking lizard that, when threatened, can suddenly produce a spiky crest. Her previous long-term partner, Gav had proved to be a wolf in sheep's clothing in wolf's clothing. Who knew what layers Calum would reveal? She did have doubts about the whole enterprise, however. Viewed objectively, the entire scheme of pursuing a schoolgirl crush was, of course, embarrassing, especially for someone who was, to a certain extent, in the public eye, but they had hit it off and she was still attracted to him. Furthermore, it appealed to her reckless side to explore the situation that had presented itself. She would just take it one date at a time and see what developed. As well him as another...

It was clearly time to stop playing games with him now, though, and in the meantime, he would just have to sweat for a little while longer. Hopefully, he'd understand.

She dashed back into the house, threw an overnight bag together, grabbed her charger from the first place she looked and jumped into the car. She had a brief unsuccessful rummage around for the USB car lighter adaptor and set off for the M1. She had another look at the first set of lights she stopped at and then remembered that she'd transferred it to her friend's Karmann Ghia when they'd driven down to Brighton the week before, and forgotten to get it back. Maybe she could get one at the services—she'd need to stop for a coffee anyway.

She hated the first stretch of the M1; it was a soulless superslab and might as well have been a tunnel. Most motorways were incredibly dull to drive on and she had a track record of getting incredibly drowsy when driving late at night —she often had to have the windows wide open for as long as she could stand it, slap herself in the face, turn the music up really loud and sing at the top of her voice, and even that didn't work sometimes. Once, on a long Friday night journey from Hastings to York, she'd tried closing one eye at a time for a few seconds in order to rest them and it did seem to help.

Hopefully, she would have enough on her mind to keep her alert this time. Her gut told her that her dad was going to be ok, but another side of her, the superstitious side, was telling her that the worst was less likely to happen if she was anticipating it and worrying about it

She got a few miles under her belt before deciding to stop at Watford Gap services for a coffee. As she waited for the incongruously-chirpy-for-this-hour barista to rustle it up, she smiled benignly and, avoiding eye-contact, stared down at the counter as he chirped on. She watched a tiny insect heading purposefully towards the pastries. Should she squash it or let it live? When she was little, she had always spared them, believing that no one had the right to deliberately end the life of another creature. She always imagined that they had a family waiting for them back home somewhere and how it would be for her if a huge thumb just came from nowhere and permanently rubbed her out for no reason? Then, one day, it occurred to her that she might be encouraging the spread of disease. She'd seen the zoomed-in illustrations of flies vomiting on our food and heard about all the insects that fly or crawl into our noses and mouths while we sleep and rethought the whole thing.

To kill or not to kill? That was the question. She'd done it a couple of times and afterwards wasn't sure if she'd felt guilty or felt nothing at all. Or just a brief undercurrent of sadness. You always felt better about yourself if you showed mercy.

She watched the minute thing scuttle and pause, scuttle and pause. It was about the size of a pinhead. What harm could it do? So what if it was near the food? She wasn't going to play god. But perhaps she already had.

The shop that might have sold a USB lighter adaptor was closed, so she decided to give her mum a ring on a payphone. She couldn't remember her mobile number so she tried the landline. It rang several times and then suddenly she heard her dad's voice say, '*Sorry, we can't get to the phone at the moment, but please leave us a message after the tone and we'll get back to you as soon as we can.*'

Her eyes filled with tears. His natural warmth and kindness came through even in that mundane sentence, but his accent sounded stronger somehow—the way he said 'forn' and 'torn'. She'd never heard that message before—they were always in when she rang as they had a very predictable weekly routine and her mum usually kept her apprised well in advance of any alterations to their schedule.

She left a message to tell them how far she'd reached, that her phone was dead and that she hoped her dad was ok.

Her mum's absence suggested that they were still at the hospital, which probably didn't bode well. It was pretty late, but it was unlikely her mother would be asleep under the circumstances. She thought about trying to call the hospital, but decided that it was better just to get up there as fast as she could.

She walked briskly through the sepulchral car park, sipping the still-too-hot coffee as she went. She was sensitive to caffeine, so wouldn't need to worry about nodding off for the rest of the journey, but took some deep breaths of the cold night air to aid the process.

As she was getting into the car, it occurred to her that she could have a silent migraine while she was driving. She'd started to experience them about two years previously and had had about three episodes since. The first time it happened, she was being interviewed for *The Guardian* and found that she couldn't focus on the interviewer. Her face had become a sort of blur, like a Francis Bacon portrait. There were also little moving rainbow-coloured crenellations (which she later found out were called Fortification Illusions) in the corner of her vision. She then started to fear that she might be having a stroke like her father had had, as she was really struggling to think of her words and was questioning whether the names she was mentioning were the right ones. The interviewer didn't seem to notice that anything was wrong, so Maria just tried to carry on as normal, hoping that it would soon pass. Fortunately, there were only five minutes of the interview left and she got through it without anyone knowing that anything was amiss. She got outside as soon as she could afterwards and went for a walk to try to clear her head, and after about five or ten minutes she was ok. She put it down to overwork, lack of sleep and too much time spent looking at a screen and, as there didn't seem to be any permanent damage, she didn't get round to seeing a doctor until it happened again about three months later. She was then referred to a specialist and it turned out that it was a kind of migraine without a headache, usually brought on by stress, tiredness, sinus issues or neck problems, none of which she thought she suffered from. As she often did in these situations, she'd felt a mixture of relief and slight disappointment that she'd made a fuss about something relatively trivial. She also thought it better not to ask the doctor about the driving situation in view of the blurred vision when he had failed to bring it up. Apparently, there was nothing much you could do about it except alleviate the causes, but taking a half an aspirin every few days seemed to help as the only time she'd had another attack since was when she'd run out of aspirin and not got round to buying any more for a couple of weeks.

She kept some in the car now, just in case, and decided to take one when she got back in. She snapped the pill in half, chewed it into powder form and washed it down with a couple of sips of coffee. She actually quite liked the taste of it.

She started up the Mini with heavy rain dancing off the windscreen and headed on up through the night with a mixture of dread and expectation washing back and forth across her mind.

5

Saturday

As he gazed out of the window of the train down to London, Dave thought about the dreams he'd been having lately. For a while now, he'd had a recurring dream in which he saw a red tower just before something terrible happened. It was always more or less the same red-brick tower, pretty nondescript, not part of a church or anything, just standing on its own rising up out of the trees or bushes. When you saw it, you wondered what it was for—it didn't look industrial and wasn't really like a water tower—but every time it cropped up in his dream—normally to his right—the road would crumble away or he'd drive off a cliff or fall down a sink hole and wake up as he was plummeting to his death.

He dreaded seeing this red tower somewhere, so he thought that it might be better for him to look out of the window as little as possible in case one came into view, signalling impending doom—or bad luck at the very least. He'd always felt unlucky—who else would have a breakdown from briefly placing their feet flat down on a cold floor? Whenever he was faced with a fifty-fifty option, he was guaranteed to choose the wrong one—except for heads and tails, where he'd always go for heads. It had occurred to him that he was part of the unluckiest generation in history, the only generation that had been dominated by slap-happy parents while growing up, and then in adulthood weren't allowed to cuff their own little emperors and princesses around the earhole.

He had never fully articulated this to himself, but deep down, all he really craved was someone to give him a big hug and tell him how sorry they felt for him, how tough things must have been for him. If this ever happened, he feared that the huge reservoir of unexpressed emotion dammed up inside him would burst and he would just sob convulsively.

He wasn't at all religious—never had been, really—but he had a weird little superstition where he would sometimes have to make the sign of the cross in a public place to either bring good luck or prevent bad luck. Whenever it came into his head, he would have to do it no matter where he was. If nobody was looking, he could just quickly do it in the normal way, but if he was in someone's line of sight, he'd have to disguise it by first briefly scratching his forehead, followed by the middle of his chest and then in turn slightly adjusting first the left and then the right shoulder of his shirt or coat. On this occasion, there was a mother and son sitting across from him, so he'd had to perform the drawn-out version.

He'd found that doing the sign of the cross repeatedly in a steady rhythm would also help him to relax when he was trying to get to sleep. He didn't see it as a religious thing—there was something about the rhythm and the focus that seemed to make him breathe more deeply and calm him down. It felt like what he imagined yoga to feel like.

Dave had been down to London on one previous occasion to do some reconnaissance work on Anna Heron and managed to find out about a few pubs that were meant to be frequented by leftie journos. It seemed pretty clear that she never went near the office, so he was going to try the pubs again. He might have to gently ask around a bit this time, but he'd play it by ear.

He opened the paper that he'd bought at the station and flicked through looking for her latest article. Why was it always so hard to find the thing that you're looking for in a newspaper or magazine?

Eventually he found it in a different part of the paper. Why were people always fiddling about with things and moving them? His eye darted over sections of the article.

One lucky World Cup and 2 World Draws?

Oh, how it must irk the Germans when English football 'supporters' taunt them with the 'One World Cup and Two World Wars' chant when they've won three World Cups and Britain can be considered to have been losing or drawing both world wars until the Americans and Russians took over…

…A classic example of English bullshit (John Bullshit?) is the Dunkirk spirit…

…merely a hugely ignominious retreat, leaving hundreds of thousands of our troops stranded and exposed. A retreat which was salvaged by a ramshackle bunch of amateur boatmen. Hardly the stuff of military legend…

… we don't really hear much about how the Japanese kicked our butts across Southeast Asia, overrunning the colonies in double quick time or about Churchill's disastrous Norwegian campaign (which, like the Gallipoli catastrophe in WW1, he eventually got away with)….

…our so-called finest hour, the Battle of Britain, wasn't exactly a rout either— more of a plucky fending off, and roughly 20% of the pilots weren't British anyway…

It was like she was taunting him personally—as if it was aimed directly at him.

You don't talk like that about the military. You don't disrespect the fallen. Everybody knows that the British military is the finest in the world. He knew it; he had seen it firsthand. There were still a few too many public schoolboys running the show for his liking, but talk like this was tantamount to treason. Who did she think she was? The bitch. He played with the annoying little hook of broken nail that he had just noticed was protruding from his middle finger. He hated having long fingernails, but he didn't want to rip it off. There were some clippers in his toilet bag but he resisted the temptation to dig them out and cut it off.

He was so agitated that he had to get up and walk as far as he could up and down the carriages to calm down. He got a can of lager at the buffet and stood there drinking it for a while before, finally becalmed, he made his way back to his seat. Planting himself down, he took out his notebook and looked back at the most recent entries.

The majority are generally wrong—geniuses are always in the minority.

Every father is either a buffoon or ogre in his own household.

Black = bass, white = treble.

Shakespeares of the street – vernacular genius
'He couldn't fight his way out of a paper bag.'
'Like shit off a shovel.'
'He's like greased lightning.'
'I wouldn't give you the steam off my shit.'
'Bingo wings.'

Misunderstood words:
laconic = taciturn. Not slow-moving, lethargic
camaraderie = comradeship. Not group banter, bonhomie, conviviality
apeth = halfpennyworth, foolish person. Not ape-like creature
bespoke = custom-made. Not renowned or spoken highly of
hiatus = pause, break. Not pinnacle or zenith.

He wanted to write a riposte to her article, but all he could think of was the phrase, *White noise.* He looked back at the notes. He didn't always carry the book around with him, so a lot of his ideas and observations had been forgotten before he could write them down and they never seemed to come back. Ever.

He looked up from the book. He couldn't just write to order. He had to work from notes. The big problem with that, however, always lay in stringing the ideas together.

He closed the book and put it back into the pocket of his Harrington. He wasn't in the mood. Actions speak louder than words anyway and he was going to take care of her one day very soon. He put his earphones in, sank down in the seat, pulled his baseball cap down over his closed eyes and listened to music for the rest of the journey. *Unknown pleasures.*

No sooner had he closed his eyes and taken a deep breath than a sandstone church tower peeping up behind some yew trees slid by unseen across the green and pleasant countryside.

Sometimes he only had to slip into a dream for a second or two to feel refreshed. What was last night's dream about the builder with two bum cleavages about? It scared him to think that you had no control over what you dreamt about.

A dream had probably been one of the final nails in the coffin of his relationship with Beth. She'd told him only a few days before she'd moved out that she'd heard him eerily announce in his sleep:

She needs something in her back—a dagger will do...

Two days later she was gone and had moved in with the guy that he later found out she'd already been seeing for six months.

The motion of the train was starting to give him an erection. It might have been partly fuelled by the thought of his ex and her Asian maths-teacher boyfriend together. Or that combined with Anna Heron and the mission ahead? He didn't think that a case of in-transit tumescence had occurred since he'd been on holiday with his friend's family at the age of seventeen. They'd been travelling overnight through France on the back seat of a minibus being driven by his mate's dad and his resolve had been stiffened when his friend's mum lay her head on his lap to get some sleep. She must have noticed—it wasn't very flattering if she hadn't, but she gave no hint of it at all. Either she didn't notice or she was a master of discretion. Why had she chosen his lap though? Somebody must have been sitting to the other side. His mate or one of his sisters.

His nickname for his circumcised penis—and indeed all circumcised penises—was *Plunkett*. He still didn't really know why he'd been circumcised as a toddler—he'd never plucked up the courage to ask his mother about it and it was too late now. He could vaguely remember having had some pain in that area and then being in the hospital after the operation with some kind of green gauze dressing wrapped around his freshly desnooded member. That was probably his earliest memory.

His dad was circumcised too but he was sure there was no vestigial Jewish thing going on. His brother hadn't had it done. He placed the newspaper over his lap and waited for it to subside.

An hour later, with a holdall firmly in his grip and, what he hoped was,a steely glint in his eye, he strode out onto the concourse of King's Cross, through the melting pot simmering around him. It seemed to get worse every time he came down.

Things had gone too far. Way too far.

He knew his history and reckoned that the rot set in after the war. His grandad hadn't stormed the beaches of Normandy in 1944 to protect minorities and let foreigners in—quite the opposite. Then the whole EU thing had snowballed until finally Tony Blair opened the floodgates and waved everybody through. A reasonable amount of immigration was fine—the English had settled in most corners of the world after all, but they obviously needed to remain the clear majority here. Remain in control. But things had got out of hand in some areas and he felt like an alien in his own country. In his own capital.

A thousand-mile journey begins with one step.

He was feeling quite peckish, so paid through the nose for a Cornish pasty at the station and stood eating it as the flotsam and jetsam of humanity flowed around him.

He always used to feel intimidated by London, overpowered by it, but not anymore.

It was his capital and he had a stake in it as much as the next man and he also realized that there'd always been an unconscious sense of the alienation and seediness underpinning the power, glamour and glory, which, for some, added to the allure rather than undermining it. He was going to mix business with pleasure. He'd be a man about town for the day; take in a few hostelries, do a bit of this and that; keep his ear to the ground, go to the British Museum, have some fish and chips on the banks of the Thames at sunset…

It might seem like he was looking for a needle in a haystack, but he had a sneaky feeling that fate would offer something up to him. He just had to be patient and vigilant.

He walked miles that day checking out the pubs he'd been recommended—the Coach and Horses, the Blacksmith and Toffee Maker and the Old Blue Last, but it was mainly tourists or students in each one. He'd also taken in Ye Olde Cheshire Cheese, even though he knew it was no longer a journo hang out—partly because it was a Samuel Smith's pub and would therefore be cheap—and it proved to be his favourite of the lot. He'd tried to talk to the barman about where the journalists hung out these days, but he was a young guy who hadn't been working there very long and had no idea about the history of the place.

It had taken so long getting around from place to place that he also hadn't had time to go to the British Museum, and as he leaned on the granite wall of the Victoria Embankment watching the khaki waters of the Thames flow by, the enjoyment of his lukewarm fish and chips was further hampered by seagulls, one of which shat on the back of his neck, with part of the guano running down the upper part of his back like melted ice cream trickling down a child's chest at the seaside. He tried to console himself with the thought that it was good luck, even though it didn't feel that way and he knew that it was probably just some old wives' bollocks that a mother must have made up to console a similarly unfortunate bird-shit-besplattered kid once upon a time.

The nights were drawing in now and the day was ebbing away as he ascended the escalators at Temple Tube station. He thought about his sister. He'd often enjoyed reminding her on June 22nd that the nights were now starting to draw in. He could still remember the transition on her face from confusion-to-shock-to-disappointment when he'd first revelled in pointing it out. It would have been nice to be going back to her cosy flat in Camden, but he couldn't risk anyone knowing he was in town.

Rising up through the concreted earth's crust, he looked across at the faces heading down in the opposite direction. Pasty face. Dead eyes. Harelip. His eye jumped ahead to an attractive Muslim woman in a headscarf. He sometimes made a point of trying to make eye contact with them as he passed them. She was studiously ignoring his stare but as they passed each other, it struck him that it could be her.

The one image he had of her was seared on his mind, and although it seemed unlikely that she would disguise herself as a Muslim, he prided himself on his facial recognition and thought it was definitely worth following her back down the escalator to check. Maybe she was Muslim rather than Jewish—that would make sense. She'd had a little scab by her eyebrow. Perhaps someone had already caught up with her?

He didn't want to rush and draw attention to himself, so he walked only slightly more briskly than normal down the escalator and, bowing down slightly as he descended, just managed to see which direction she was heading in once he'd got halfway down. Arriving at the crowded platform, he was relieved to see that there wasn't a train just leaving.

He had a calm, slow-motion glance either side of him and spotted her about twenty-five yards to his left, standing back close to the wall. She looked different from that angle and doubt that it was actually her started to creep in, but he reassured himself that people can look very different in profile.

When they got onto the crowded train, he was able to position himself about fifteen yards to her right and slightly behind her. He thought he detected a flicker of amusement playing on her lips as she looked at the London 2012 poster opposite her. Dave was convinced there would be a terror attack at some point during the games. It was inevitable— they'd be hellbent on spoiling the party. He pretended to be studying the Tube map opposite him, but as each stop approached, he made sure to keep her in his peripheral vision in case she made to get off.

He pulled the visor of his baseball cap down over his eyes a little—not too much. He now considered himself to be on active service and the heaving, hybrid humanity around him might as well not have been there. A frenzy of flames could have consumed them all and he would scarcely have noticed.

When she got off, so did he. Along the grubby, tiled, intestinal tunnels they went, onto the escalator, across the concourse and finally up the steps until they emerged back out onto the streets of London like two actors coming up through the trap door of a stage, but with the autumn chill caressing their ears rather than the warmth of the footlights.

Dave had followed people before, but only random people. He'd followed them to their homes or wherever, mainly for the thrill of knowing that they were oblivious to the fact that they were being followed. As they turned into their garden paths and blithely slotted their keys into the locks of their front doors, he'd wander past, usually on the other side of the street, revelling in the fact that they had no idea what was going on, that this dark stranger, a mere extra in their lives, had secretly homed in on them.

He saw himself as like an animal in the wild. Always alert, on its guard, looking around in every direction for potential threats. That was nature's way.

This seemed to go against the fact that he had a sneaking suspicion that he might be immortal—not immortal in the sense that he was immune to violence, but rather in the sense that he couldn't see himself ever dying of an illness or natural causes. He felt as if he could go on forever if he could just stay clear of mortal danger.

There were a lot of nutters out there and you needed to Keep Your Wits About You. That was his motto— KYWAY. *KYWAY on the highway*. It was a fight for survival and you were an idiot if you thought that you could just breeze through life thinking the best of people. Life was competitive. All animals were competing for resources. Vigilance was required at all times.

The other aspect of trailing people that appealed to him was that no crime had been committed—it was a one-off each time and all he was doing was simply taking a walk— and there wasn't even the intention of committing a crime. He never followed the same person more than once and to all intents and purposes, it was just a stroll.

This was different, however, this was targeted, but still, there was absolutely nothing linking him to her.

The woman he strongly suspected of being Anna Heron was striding about twenty-five yards up ahead. In his eyes, the self-contained, aloof demeanour of her prim rear end in black jeans abstractly echoed the proud, self-important look he'd seen on her face.

It would make sense for her to be heading home at this time and when she emerged from an organic mini-mart with a carrier bag of groceries, his hopes seemed to be confirmed.

He'd replaced his cap with a beanie hat and crossed the street while she was in there and, under the guise of examining a curry house menu, was watching the reflection of the mini-mart entrance in the window as he waited for her to emerge.

They were entering just the sort of area he'd expected her to live in. Handsome townhouses with plenty of Volvos and Saabs parked around. He kept about thirty yards back on the other side of the road until she turned sharply into a side street. Casually quickening his pace until he could see down the street, he hoped she hadn't disappeared into one of the first gardens.

The pavement was empty. Momentary panic, but then he saw her emerge from behind a van on the other side of the road. She continued on past house after house as the road rose and arced round to the left until she slipped between two tall stone gateposts that were leaning out over the pavement slightly.

He hung back a little until he heard the front door close then walked past the gateposts, made a mental note of the house number—sixty-six— and which floors didn't yet have their lights on—top and middle—and then continued on up to the end of the street.

He pretended to study the menu in a Chinese restaurant window on the corner of the other end of the street, unconsciously taking in the strangely purposeful tropical fish in the window aquarium. He took out a cigarette, flipped his Zippo lighter open and stared into the orange, gravity-defying tongue of flame for several seconds. He felt a curious urge to quickly dart his own tongue in and out of the flame without feeling it, but quickly thought better of it, lit a cigarette and snapped the lighter lid shut as if he was reloading a rifle. He put his cap back on, took out a scarf from his jacket pocket, threw it student-style around his neck, noted the name of the street—Maimie Road—and headed back down towards number sixty-six, deliberately walking with a limp and taking pleasure in each lungful of smoke. *It was happening—he was crossing the Rubicon.*

He was vaguely aware of a background gut feeling trying to put the brakes on things, but another stronger, more central compulsion was overriding it. It was all about crossing lines—that's what made heroes heroes and that's what he'd always felt he was destined to be. It had just been a matter of time. The treble was drowning out the bass. The arrow was in flight.

Both the ground and middle floors now had their lights on and, fortunately, the curtains were closed on both. Treading softly, as casually as he could, he padded up the short path to look at the doorbell pad in the vague hope that there would be a possible name for her by the middle flat doorbell. The ground floor flat said *Torvill and Dean*—obviously a pair of jokers—but the other two flats had no name. For FFF, it looked as if a blank sticker had been stuck over another one, so he shone his phone torch on it and could just about make out a faded name that seemed to say *Anna Aharoni*.

That must be her real name. It must be her. It would be much too much of a coincidence.

He quickly headed back down the garden path, only half suppressing the spring in his step. *Through fires of death we walk.*

He felt invincible as he turned, looked down at his phone and thinking, *This calls for a well-earned pint and a spot of online research,* stepped sideways between two cars to cross the road.

20

Calum was sitting outside 58 Maimie Road in his hazelnut Saab. Rachel had insisted on calling it 'the brown car' or 'the diarrhoeamobile', even though he'd tried to show her on the DVLA registered keeper certificate that it was officially described as hazelnut. She'd declined to look, of course.

He'd decided that it was fitting that Anna should continue to benefit from his anonymous-kindness-to-strangers programme. The whole thing about Ally's address in Australia was also nagging away at him too. It all just seemed too much of a coincidence. His enthusiasm for the enterprise had also been renewed since Maria had blown him out on the date. He couldn't stop thinking about her and would oscillate from feeling like he was smitten with the most amazing woman he'd ever met to feeling as if he were in the depths of humiliation, anger and confusion. It wasn't the hope that was killing him, the hope that there would turn out to be a perfectly reasonable explanation for why she'd disappeared, it was the moments of hope that were sustaining him, but he needed to do something to take his mind off the moments of despair and expend his surplus nervous energy. He also didn't have the girls this weekend as they had gone to Rachel's mum's seventieth birthday do.

Having decided that he was actually going to follow something through for once rather than just talk about it, he still wasn't sure, however, what form his altruism should take. He'd bought one of Maria's books that morning and this was also spurring him on.

His car had needed picking up from its MOT and service in Anna's vague part of town so he thought he'd check out where she lived to see if that would give him any ideas of what other good turn he could do for her. He also had the vague, consciously ridiculous idea that if he drove around a bit, fate might just throw up Maria.

He'd also heard that there'd been a couple of sexual assaults in that part of the city and the thought that he might notice something suspicious and even be able to thwart the attacker failed to override the paranoid thought that it might not be wise to hang around there in case he became implicated in something.

It occurred to him that he shouldn't have put his name on the note accompanying the purse, and started to feel uncomfortable about being there. He reminded himself that the bottom line was that he hadn't done anything wrong and wasn't planning to do anything wrong—but the whole concept suddenly now began to feel ill-conceived. What the hell was he thinking of, doing little favours and treats for the privileged? Hadn't this all been basically done before in *Amélie* anyway? He should be out there helping the homeless or volunteering at a community kitchen or youth centre or something.

As he sat in the car shaking his head at what a fool he was, a message notification came up on the dating app. It was from Maria.

So very sorry about the other night. Did you get the message from the barman? While you were in the loo, I got a call from my mum saying that my dad had been rushed to hospital and it didn't look good. The battery on my phone went mid-call and I just had to rush up North there and then. Fortunately, it looks as if he's going to be OK, but it was touch and go for a while and that's why I didn't contact you.

I was having a lovely time the other night btw. Assuming my dad comes out of hospital and continues to make good progress, we could meet up again next week when I get back to London—in the unlikely event that you've forgiven me by then that is?

I've got a secret to reveal... My number's not 0203 1 9 18 1 13 btw (They fell backwards in Porto). It's

07992983441… Resistance is useless? Sorry again, Maria x

Calum looked up from his phone out into the fading light and then down at the message again. He fumbled for a pen and scrap of paper in the doorwell and wrote the word CAIRAM and then reversed it—MARIAC.

Maria C.

Maria C…

Maria Cormack.

There was a Maria Corr in his English class. She went to St Boniface's too. She was really good at playing the guitar. She could play that Mexican Hat Dance tune while he was badly strumming along to *On top of Old Smokey.* Her fingernails used to be badly bitten back.

Even though she had been in a lot of the same classes as him, he couldn't remember ever speaking to her that much at St Bede's, but he remembered her as a smart, knowing presence hanging around in the background with her best friend, Anne-Marie Price.

She looked very different, but it could be her. He hadn't noticed the fingernails but they surely wouldn't still be like that anyway.

Same dark hair and blue eyes though. He remembered that sometimes he'd see her and Anne-Marie smiling at him and couldn't decide if they were taking the mick out of him or not. She always looked like she was quietly navigating the corridors of secondary school, biding her time until she could make her way in the world that mattered. He caught the flash of the look that she'd been giving him when he'd started talking about writing. It was the same look.

Bloody hell, it *was* her. *Jesus.* Well, well, well…

He reread the message and just as his finger was poised above the keyboard to reply, he suddenly felt the front of the car jolt and heard a sickening crunch and growl of pain. He looked up and saw a lantern-jawed man with a hook nose and dark moustache lurch sideways on to his bonnet in agony and look him directly in the eye for an instant.

'What the...?'

The guy then slithered off the bonnet as the car in front pulled forwards again.

As Calum was jumping out of the car to help him, the driver of the car in front was doing the same.

'I'm sorry. He can't have heard me reversing. It's an electric car.'

As he came round to the back of the car, you could see him realise that he hadn't turned his lights on.

The injured party was groaning and grimacing on the ground. His knees looked twisted in an unnatural position.

'Shit. I'll phone an ambulance.'

As he was doing that, Calum tried to remember his first aid training.

1. Reassure him.

'It's OK mate, the ambulance is on its way. You're going to be OK.'

There were two mnemonics: DR.ABC and AMPLE.

D was for danger—make sure the scene is safe. Get the driver to check whether the handbrakes are on when he comes off the phone.

The guy on the ground was conscious, but obviously couldn't stand up so Calum just tried to make him as comfortable as possible between the two cars.

He adjusted the askew baseball cap on his head to give him a bit of comfort and loosened the university-style scarf he was wearing.

Calum was worried that he might go into shock and he couldn't properly remember how you responded to that.

He did remember that you needed to continue to talk to them, so he introduced himself and asked the guy his name—Dave—and told him that he was a first aider and the ambulance wouldn't be long. The patient was conscious, so he could skip most of DR. ABC. C was for circulation. Was he bleeding? He looked along his body—he didn't seem to be.

He couldn't remember what the A in AMPLE stood for but M was for medication. So, he asked him if he was on any medication—he wasn't.

The driver was describing the guy's condition to the person on the phone.

P? Previous medical history.

'Have you got any medical conditions the medics will need to know about?'

'Does a broken heart count?'

L was last meal. How long since your last meal?

'Lunchtime—about half one.'

The flat vowel sounds suggested he was from up north.

'You don't sound like you're from round here, Dave. Where are you from?'

'Near Scunthorpe.'

'That's Yorkshire, isn't it?'

'Lincolnshire.'

'Well, you're going to be OK. It won't be long now.'

E. What was E for?

The other driver had come off the phone and seemed to be in more of a panic than Dave.

'I didn't see you park up. There wasn't anyone behind me when I got in and then my wife rang saying that one of the kids had a temperature and could I pick up some Calpol on the way back.'

'Don't worry, mate. These things happen. Can you just check that we've both put our hand brakes on?'

A couple of the neighbours had come out by this point to see what was going on.

One of them, an attractive thirty-something woman in a headscarf with her arms folded against the evening chill, saw Dave lying there.

'Oh my God, what happened?'

Calum recognized her immediately from her ID card.

'This guy accidentally reversed into him.'

He refrained from adding, '*and his legs got crushed between the two cars.*'

'Oh dear. Is there anything I can do?'

'No, I think we're OK, thanks. That might be our ambulance that we can hear.'

Just then her phone rang and she said,

'Sorry, I'd better take this,' and started to withdraw towards her gate.

'Oh hi Gavin… Good, thanks… No, it's fine, I'm just outside the flat— a guy has been hit by a car… He's OK, I think. They're just waiting for the ambulance. Hang on a sec.'

She put her hand over the receiver, turned to Calum and said,

'I hope he's going to be OK.'

Nodding solemnly in pursed-lipped acknowledgement, Calum almost blurted out, 'It was me that sent your purse back.'

Still on the phone, Anna headed back inside.

Dave seemed to be calming down, as if he was resigned to whatever fate awaited him.

'I know at the end of the day that nothing really matters, but I can't help getting worked up about stuff.'

'It's OK, mate, you're going to be alright. Just take it easy.'

The ambulance and the police arrived in quick succession. As Dave was carefully lifted on to a stretcher, Calum noticed that the back of his head was matted with blood. He must have hit his head as he fell when the car in front jerked forward to release him.

He looked as if he was drifting away into unconsciousness as they carried him into the ambulance. Eventually, the doors slammed shut and the ambulance headed off into the night, its siren call drifting in and out of earshot on the evening breeze.

The police took statements from him and the other driver, who seemed resigned to the worst, and then finally, they exchanged details in case some internal damage to the Saab came to light— doubtful with that old warhorse, but you never knew.

When Calum eventually got back into his car, he heaved a ragged sigh of relief and looked back out towards Anna's house.

He had no idea how long he'd been there and looked at the time on his watch.

6.30pm.

The crocodile seemed to be laughing, but this time with him, rather than at him.

He took out his phone, read Maria's message again and started to type.

Hi Maria, very sorry to hear about your dad. I hope you're coping ok. I completely understand. I can't believe I didn't realize that it was you. What a dark (sea)horse!

I had a great time too and would love to meet up again. Resistance is indeed useless and I have definitely taken a fall.

He paused. Should he leave the last bit in? It could all still be a game.

He continued,

I'll ring you in a couple of days or you can ring me in the meantime if you feel up to it – 07922814688. We've got some catching up to do. Calum x

He pored over every word, deleting and then more often than not, reinserting the same thing here and there until, ten minutes later, he sent the message.

He looked across at Anna's house again through the trees and then back to the space where the Prius had been parked in front of him and smiled as he remembered what the E in AMPLE was for —*Event history*.

A few windblown raindrops smattered across the windscreen. He looked down at the buttons on his dark blue coat, twitched involuntarily, then started up the engine and sat for a few moments listening to it turning over.

Up above, through the trees, Anna peered out of the curtains to see whether the police car had now gone and saw Calum pulling away in the Saab. It was closely followed by an unmarked car which had been parked several spaces behind. Though she craned her neck, she couldn't see far enough around the bend in the road to know whether it had turned in the same direction or not at the junction. She felt an urge to continue standing there staring out at nothing for a while, and then catching the ghost of her reflection in the window, let the curtain fall and turned back inside.

Coda

The day drawing to a close, a herring gull glides over the rooftops and roads, banking here and there as necessary. An occasional nonchalant flap of wing is all that is required to propel her towards the Suffolk shores to rejoin the flock and bed down for the night.

With the sunset behind her, she casts a dispassionate eye across the schools, the offices, the town houses, the trees, telegraph poles and teetering towers; the roads, canals, bridges and railways; the well-being women rolling up their mats by Wellington Arch, the mandarin peeved to be summoned to Whitehall at the weekend and the would-be poet crossing Westminster bridge—all the irrelevant, earth-bound fringe beneath.

She would soon be resting and then perhaps tomorrow, as the autumn chill creeps in, the gulls will turn their heads once again, as they do each year, and fly south across the Bay of Biscay to the sands of Galicia, before winging onwards, skirting the Portuguese coastline, until, a month or two later, they arrive on the shores of Morocco.

Next spring, the call will come and she will turn to rise again and wheel once more, northwards along the same winding route past Isla da Canela, Vilanova de Milfontes and Montijo, over Morgat and Île-Molène and on to Maiden Castle before alighting on Marble Arch to cast a cold eye on the magisterial masses and quickening clouds once again.

Appendix

A poem by David King

I am Winter

Bleached heart
heart in brine
burnt heart
burnt alive
Can anyone smell burning?

The head survives,
thrives and flies
underground
in the fullness of time
being what it ought to be,
in due course.

Head in a box,
headlong
head-led,
dispatched
into the infinite,
blank expanses,
blank verse
of whiteout.

Selected extracts from the articles of Anna Heron

One lucky World Cup and 2 World Draws?

Oh, how it must irk the Germans when English football supporters taunt them with the 'One World Cup and Two World Wars Chant' when they themselves have won three World Cups and Britain, at best, can be considered to have been drawing both world wars until the Americans and Russians took over…

Since that glorious afternoon for Sir Alf and the boys in July 1966, the aggregate score for West Germany/Germany is thirteen wins to the Germans and five for the plucky English, which must make it all the more galling for our Teutonic cousins. (England fans note to self: must learn how not to rile opponents into outperforming us quite so much).

Following our latest comprehensive humbling by the German national football team in this summer's South African World Cup and yet another premature exit from an international tournament, the recent announcement by the FA that it intends to revert to an English manager after Euro 2012 raises the obvious question of whether that's such a clever idea given the track record of English managers over the last fifty years.

It also leads us to consider the calibre of English management across society as a whole and through history. We like to think of ourselves as practical, pragmatic people with common sense who <u>can</u> organise a piss up in a brewery, but do the facts bear this out?

Rather than the stout yeomanry of yore, are England now the national equivalent of the cocky, mouthy schoolboy who covers up for his lack of knowledge about anything much by messing about at the back of the class, making a few of his classmates snigger?

As we're talking about football and Germany, what else springs to the English mind but matters military, so let's start there, shall we?

A classic example of English bullshit (John Bullshit?) is the Dunkirk spirit. Granted, a lot of ordinary citizens acted bravely in getting thousands of troops home safely, but, viewed in another light, you could maybe conclude that it was basically a hugely ignominious retreat, leaving hundreds of thousands of our troops stranded and exposed on a foreign shore. A retreat which was salvaged by a ramshackle bunch of amateur boatmen because the armed forces were incapable of doing it themselves. Hardly the stuff of military legend, nicht wahr?

Staying with WW2, we don't really hear much about how the Japanese kicked our asses (or donkeys?) across Southeast Asia, overrunning the colonies in double-quick time. Or about Churchill's disastrous Norwegian campaign (which, like the Gallipoli catastrophe in WW1, he eventually got away with).

Even our so-called finest hour, the Battle of Britain, wasn't exactly a rout— more of a plucky fending off, and roughly 20% of the pilots weren't British anyway.

Going further back in time… If you asked the average English person about previous battles with France, they are likely to bring up Agincourt, not realizing that that was one of the few high points in an unsuccessful campaign that eventually resulted in the loss of all England's French territories—which made up roughly half of the country—apart from the Channel Islands. Ultimately, it was our Gallic cousins flicking us the Agincourt archer Vs as we slithered back to our 'sceptered isle' (old Bill Shakes was obviously not too hot on English geography or maybe he just thought 'sceptered half an island' didn't scan as well)

Others might mention Waterloo, but that was very much a joint effort with the Prussians and Dutch, and only 25,000 of the 118,000 troops taking to the field against the greatly outnumbered French that day were British. Furthermore, the hero of the hour, the Duke of Wellington, who gets full credit on our side of the Channel for the victory—there being little mention of the Prussian commander, von Blücher— was— although he was, famously and shamefully, in denial about it—actually Irish.

Of course, it hasn't all been failure or mitigated victory. There have been genuinely great victories in winning campaigns such as Trafalgar—though even then our head honcho hero Horatio did get himself killed—but it seems that for every El-Alamein, there is a Charge of the Light Brigade or Saratoga...

The Untied Kingdom

... Britain will never approach anything near the greatness it's always banging on about until it is properly united and has an authentic sense of its own identity.

Contrary to popular belief, it is we English who hold the keys to keeping the grand old U of K together and unless we change tack pretty soon, Scotland and then Wales and Northern Ireland will go their separate ways, especially if, as seems increasingly likely, the Prime Minister bows to his Eurosceptics and risks the patriacide of taking us out of Europe.

The English have long told themselves that the main obstacle to unity is the resentful attitude of the Celtic fringe, who are simply jealous of England's superior success, power and wealth, and like nothing better than to see the Sassenachs fail. To my eyes, however, it is more the arrogance and patrician attitude of the little Englanders that is continuing to widen the cracks. Celtic eyes, on the whole, rather than being green with envy, see England as a bit of an arrogant, deluded underachiever when you take its relative wealth and population into account.

This Anglo-Saxon high-handedness can be seen in the many unrectified historical, political and cultural oversights, such as the fact that there is no Welsh *representation in the Union flag or the Royal Standard (in the latter there is, bafflingly— and to add insult to injury— another set of three lions {or are they leopards?}—where the Welsh dragon should be).*

I could also point to the fact that the UK cricket team is simply called England—although they might have Welsh, Scottish or Irish players alongside the customary South African or two. Sometimes, however, we English don't even need to point out that an organisation is English at all, as it is, of course, the original and definitive one of its kind. Take the FA for example. We're so special that we don't need to say the English FA. Just the FA will do, thank you very much! They're probably tempted to put the 'the' in italics too, just in case some of us didn't get the message. Not surprisingly, the UK golf establishment takes a similarly humble approach by sticking with the name 'the Open' rather than 'the British Open.'

We don't even bother to put the name of our country on our stamps either. Why should we? We're not an ordinary country like everyone else...

The playing of the British national anthem before England football and rugby games against the other home nations is further evidence of this John Bull-in-a-china-shop syndrome that we seem all too oblivious of...

Why isn't England a country?

...It strikes me that two of the main prerequisites to qualify as a country must surely be:

> *A.   a passport*
> *B.   a Prime Minister or President*

The last time I checked, England had neither. Scotland, Wales and Northern Ireland have, in a way, stronger claims to being countries as at least they have their own parliaments/assemblies and de facto Prime Ministers, but, at the end of the day, they are all, at best, pseudo countries and only really considered to be countries due to the creation of separate 'national' sporting teams.

This, of course, is wonderful as a focus of regional pride and rivalry, but is a huge own goal in terms of UK-level national unity. Other major European countries such as Germany, France and Italy, which are also made up of a number of separate historic kingdoms or city states, have wisely avoided going down the route that we have taken and are laughing into their Riesling, Merlot and Chianti that we choose to conveniently undermine ourselves by dividing into four smaller units.

If Italy had separate Lombardy, Tuscany, Sicily and Sardinia football teams, they almost certainly wouldn't have won three world cups between them as the united Italian team has managed to do.

Of course, in typical John Bullshit fashion, we try to get round the conundrum of how the UK and each of its constituent parts can all be countries by referring to England, Scotland, Wales and Northern Ireland as the four nations. How exactly is a nation different to a country then? Does the British PM not address the nation, when he speaks in public? Does the UK not belong to an international institution called the United Nations?

Let's face it, they're regions and to suggest anything else is just deluded. Having a flag doesn't make a nation. If it did, it would mean that Dorset, Selfridges and my local Toyota dealership would all be joining Ban Ki-moon at his next pow wow...

...At the end of the day, maybe we're simply a quarrelsome, divisive people, who just like to define ourselves by what we're not,

Sorry to come back to football again, but it is our 'national' sport after all... Just look at how many professional teams there are in London compared to Paris, Madrid, Rome or Berlin. In case you're wondering, there are twelve. Twelve! You're hard-pressed to reach three in the other major European capitals. And if we take a little *tour round the country, the majority of our cities have two teams that usually reserve their greatest contempt for their nearest neighbours.*

Of course, there is strong enmity between the rival teams in cities around Europe, but it seems particularly pronounced here in dear old Blighty. Why is this? We don't seem that keen on Johnny Foreigner, but why do we love to hate each other so much?

Milton Keynes UK
Ingram Content Group UK Ltd.
UKHW050744280324
440234UK00014B/233

9 781835 631638